W9-BUW-950

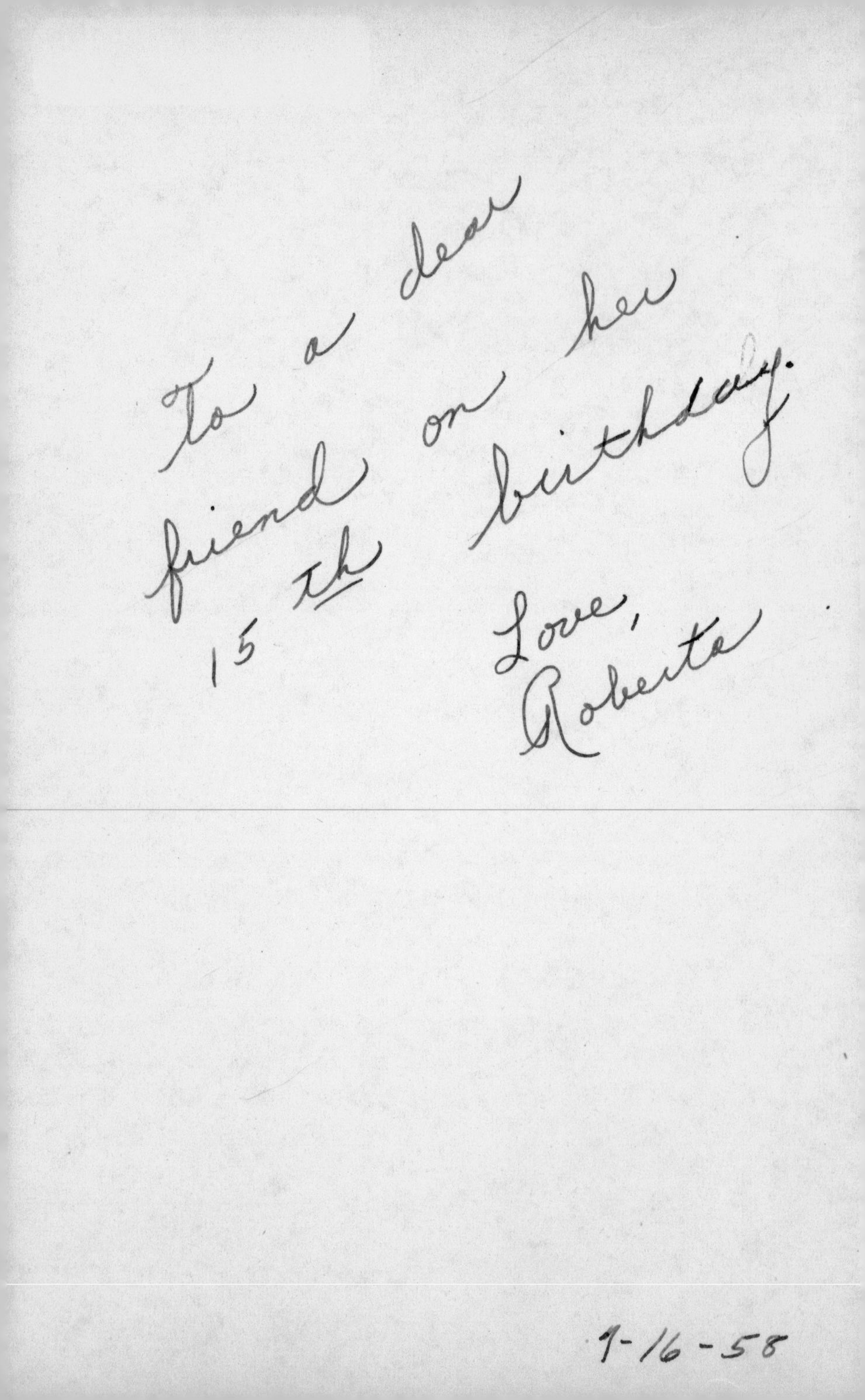

To a dear
friend on her
15 th birthday.

Love,
Roberta

9-16-58

NIGHT TRAIN TO SCOTLAND

NIGHT TRAIN TO SCOTLAND

by Sybil Burr

THE WESTMINSTER PRESS

Philadelphia

NIGHT TRAIN TO SCOTLAND was first published by Routledge & Kegan Paul, Ltd., in England under the title *Lantern of the North.*

Library of Congress Catalog Card Number: 56-5108

PRINTED IN THE UNITED STATES OF AMERICA

THIS BOOK IS FOR
CHARLES AND BARBARA BAIN
AND THEIR SONS
DAVID AND BILLY
OF INVERNESS

I would like to thank Phebe Snow for the support and encouragement she gave me while I was writing this book. Also the many friends to whom I never went in vain when I needed factual help. In particular, Bee and Charlie in Inverness, Ramsgate Public Library, and Mr. H. W. Hazlewood who read the proofs.

1

NIGHT TRAIN TO SCOTLAND

THE rattle and racket of King's Cross Station on a hot July evening, with the surging tide of holidaymakers churning in and out of the airless waiting room. . . .

"You can say what you like, Elsie," remarked an elderly waitress who stood with her back against the doors of the Refreshment Room, "I think holidays is overrated. Just look at that crowd. All milling to and fro and struggling and heaving like a lot of ants. Just so as they can get to some beach or other and mill and struggle and heave there."

"You're thinking of Waterloo where you was before," replied Elsie. "You don't get that kind of beach at the end of journeys from King's Cross. Mostly rain and heather and men running after deers and things, isn't it? Sounds a bit dreary to me, Gert."

"That nice young feller in Naval uniform we had in the Buffit just now didn't look as if he was going to find it dreary."

"Did you see the sticky buns he put away? A day like this too!"

"I also see the bob he gave me," observed Gert. "There he goes! Look! He's eating again. Sweets this time. Good luck to him, I say. Wish I was young and fresh as the heather he's going to."

Holly Gordon was eagerly scanning the contents of the bookstall.

"Oh, look, Aunt Lottie! Here's *The Hooded Horror Strikes Again*. I haven't read that one."

Miss Charlotte Gordon pursed her lips and glanced disapprovingly at the picture of a green and purple hand grasping a dagger.

"I think at fifteen it is time you were growing out of that kind of literature," she said severely, with yet the hint of a twinkle in her eye. "Now what about this? *The Concise Guide to Current Affairs*. I don't expect it's as dull as it sounds."

"There shouldn't be such things as current affairs in July and August! We have enough of them in civics at school! And they're terrible!" protested Holly, rolling her eyes. "They always send me to sleep!"

"Then I should have thought they were the best thing to read in a sleeping car," commented her aunt, putting down the eightpence for *The Hooded Horror Strikes Again*. "I'd better just check your sleeping berth at the office. We don't want any muddle."

"You've checked it twice already," said Holly, laughing. "They'll think you don't trust them."

"They'd think right," replied her aunt. "And I don't like the idea of your traveling on your own all that way, either. It's what comes of having a fly-by-night like my brother for a father."

"Daddy's not a fly-by-night! He's a most respectable headmaster. And an M.A. and a F.Z.S."

"Fellow of the Zoological Society!" snorted Miss Gordon, pushing Holly's ticket under her glove. " Birds, birds, birds! And when it isn't birds, it's cutting flowers up sideways and impaling harmless insects on bits of cork. I wonder he has any control over his schoolboys at all. And your mother with her head always full of burnt umber and chrome yellow or whatever she calls those squashy paint tubes of hers! "

Several people turned and smiled at Holly's laughing face with its cap of fair hair.

" Though they haven't made such a bad job of you," conceded Miss Gordon, " in spite of their various madnesses. It's nearly seven o'clock. I think we ought to get you settled in. I just hope you arrive safely."

" I'll be into Fort William at six minutes past ten tomorrow morning," declared Holly. " Mother and Daddy are meeting me there."

" Yes, I know they are," said Miss Gordon grimly. " If they don't forget all about you, that is."

She led the way through the barrier, treated the ticket inspector to a regal nod, and swept toward the Fort William sleeping car.

" D4," she said. " Look for D4, Holly. I do hope there'll be some nice people in the other bunks who'll keep an eye on you. Such strange people seem to be able to afford to travel on sleepers nowadays. Now do remember to stay in the Fort William car and don't go wandering about the corridors. Your coaches will be taken off at Edinburgh and if you're not in them, you'll be carried on to Aberdeen or some outlandish place in the back of beyond where it's all bog and water. I don't approve of Scotland. It has far too much rain and far too few roads. Bournemouth would have been so much simpler."

Holly opened the door of the sleeping car. " This is it,"

she said. " Oh, good! I've got a bottom bunk."

Miss Gordon peered cautiously into the compartment and glanced at the neatly folded gray blanket and clean pillow. Two elderly faces appeared for a moment around the covers of two books in the upper bunks.

" Good evening," remarked Miss Gordon graciously at the covers of the two books. " Put the suitcase under your bunk, Holly. And be sure to make those sandwiches last as far as Fort William. I've made you a caraway-seed cake and there's a bottle of that terrible fizzy stuff I know you like in the box."

She handed Holly the ticket. " Now get settled and stay settled, there's a good child."

Holly sat down on D4 and thumped the pillow.

" Don't worry, Aunt," she grinned. " It isn't the first time I've done this journey on my own. I'll creep under the blanket and pretend I'm not here."

Miss Gordon snorted. " What! " she said. " A girl your size! Five foot six and one hundred and twenty-five pounds. . . ."

She stopped speaking suddenly. Her eye had alighted upon a nautical cap with its white linen cover lying in the corner of the other lower bunk.

" The Navy! " said Miss Gordon. " The Navy is most respectable. Probably some nice old sea captain who'll take care of you and talk boats. Where is he, though? It's practically a quarter past seven."

" Seeing his luggage in, I expect," said Holly. " Oh, Aunt, do get out quickly! There's the first whistle. Unless you want to come with me, of course."

Miss Gordon bundled hurriedly onto the platform and Holly let down the corridor window.

" Here's something for you to spend on yourself, darling," said her aunt, looking up into the smiling gray eyes

with unusual warmth. " Don't let your father borrow it."

Holly stared at the ten-shilling note and then at Miss Gordon's thin face and well-worn felt hat.

" Aunt Lottie, you are sweet! But you can't spare it, I'm sure! Please don't give it to me."

" Take it while I've still got it to give, my dear," Miss Gordon said dryly. " There's the flag. You're off. Mind you write to me from that little island of yours."

The seven-fifteen King's Cross to Aberdeen began to jerk slowly along the platform. Miss Gordon was left waving at the fair head hanging out of the corridor window.

Holly waved until a curve in the track cut off her view of the ancient felt hat. She tossed back her hair and stared eagerly up the line through the flying engine grit.

The two elderly persons in the top bunks were glaring disapprovingly at the smoke pouring in through the open window.

" ' Beyond the blue horizon dawns a bee-utiful day,' " yelled Holly suddenly and, re-entering the compartment, meekly shut the door. She sank down on her bunk and opened the food box.

" M'mmmm. Sardine sandwiches," she murmured to herself. " Just one little one, I think, and then no more until we reach the border. I wonder if I dare take off my skirt and put my shorts on."

She eyed the respectable scene as the train rolled through Harringay and then glanced doubtfully up at the two recumbent figures.

" Not yet, I think. I'll endure it as far as Berwick and directly we get into Scotland off comes my skirt."

The last of the sardine sandwiches had by now been consumed and her energy had returned. She got up and inspected the nautical cap of the ancient sea captain.

" A crest with a crown on it," muttered Holly. " He

might be in the dining car. Not already though, surely. Perhaps he isn't used to trains. Perhaps he's got locked in the luggage van."

All Holly's detective instincts, born of a close study of the methods of the Hooded Horror, rose to the surface. She opened the door of the compartment.

The corridor was empty except for a figure farther up, leaning with both arms across the rail. Now what is he? she thought. An old boy or a young man? An old boy, I think.

The boy turned his head and glanced at Holly.

"Hey!" she hissed urgently, "there's a poor old captain gone and lost himself on this train. I'm frightfully worried."

"Which way did he go?" the boy said, taking his arms from the rail and coming toward her. "A friend of yours?"

"Sort of," said Holly. "I was hoping we'd be able to talk boats. I don't really want to miss the chance. If I don't hurry up and find him, he'll be turning in for the night and that'll be that."

"I see," the boy said. "Well, let's start working toward the luggage van."

Holly glanced up at him gratefully. He's very good-looking, she thought. And he doesn't look Londonish, thank goodness. He's too brown and smells of the open air.

"You go first," she said. "I'm Holly Gordon. And thanks very much — " She hesitated.

"Ross Mordley," the boy said, smiling down at her. "How d'you do, Holly."

The train had shaken off the back yards and was now streaming at speed toward the open country. Holly swayed after Ross toward the next coach.

"You've got a real old Scots name," she commented hopefully. "You Scots?"

"Don't really know," Ross said, peering into a com-

partment, much to the annoyance of the occupants who were settling down for the night. " It's a sort of family name. I believe my ancestors came from Scotland. My great-great-grandfather was a pirate."

Holly stared at his auburn hair as she staggered along after him.

" I don't believe you," she shouted above the thunder of the wheels. " How many greats did you say? There aren't such things as pirates."

" There were when the old Villain was around," Ross yelled back. " What's this seafaring type of yours look like? "

" Don't know," Holly replied. " I've only met his cap. It's the Navy kind with a linen cover and a crest with a crown on it."

Ross stopped. " On one of the bottom bunks in sleeping car D? " he asked.

" How did you know? " Holly demanded. Ross burst out laughing. " We've found him," he grinned. " We've been looking for me."

Holly glared at his navy-blue uniform and noticed the same crown on the buttons.

" But you're not an ancient sea captain! "

" No, and I shan't even be a second mate for at least four years. But I can talk boats if you want to. Look, let's go and have a coffee and I'll explain."

They staggered back to the dining car and sat down.

" It's like this," Ross said. " I'm a Merchant Navy cadet at the School of Navigation. At least, I was. I've just finished my forty week's training. I've now arrived at the ripe old age of seventeen and a half and waiting for my first ship."

Holly looked at him and noticed for the first time his curiously amber-colored eyes. Eyes that lightened to a

clear gold when he smiled.

" Your first ship? " she said. " Are you really going to sea? "

" Just as soon as the Oceanic Shipping Company sends for me," Ross said. " You see, when you get to the intermediate class, the director sends around a list and you choose which shipping line you'd like to serve with. I got the pick of the lot because — "

" Go on," said Holly.

" Because I was one of the cadet captains."

" Do you have to be awfully clever to be a cadet captain? " asked Holly.

Ross stared into his cup. " You have to — well, you know, get pretty good marks."

Holly sighed. " I'm not a bit clever. I'll just die if I don't get into the W.R.N.S. I've been crazy about it for two whole years. All our Sea Ranger Crew's aiming at the W.R.N.S. Daddy's got a sort of boat. Pretty ramshackle but it goes and that's the main thing. Daddy's coming up Loch Linnhe to meet me at Fort William and pick up the stores. If he remembers, that is. Are you on the way to join your ship? "

" Steady on! " Ross laughed. " They don't work as fast as all that! I may have to wait two or three months. I've left my address with Mrs. Todd. She's my landlady. I lost my dad in 1950. Can't even remember my mother. That's how I got into the School of Navigation. On a grant, I mean. They take you cheaper if your father was killed at sea."

Holly was silent. Then she put out her hand across the table. " I'm sorry, Ross. Bragging about my father. Does it cost a lot to be a cadet? "

" Too much unless you do something about it before-

hand," Ross smiled. " A paper route before school. Delivering groceries between school and homework. Anything I could get. It took me three years to raise the cash. I've always been set on the Merchant Navy. My dad was first officer in the *Portland Bay*. He jumped into the sea to pick up a seaman who'd gone overboard in the Indian Ocean. The propeller got him."

They were both silent for a few minutes.

Then Ross said, " Ever done any acting, Holly? "

" Only in school plays," she replied. " Why? "

" Some of us met a Major and Mrs. Lumley at Southampton. They're good sports but a bit cracked. Especially over the theater. They dash about the country giving shows with an old caravan trailer they've got. I went around Dorset playing the junior lead and camping in a tent for a couple of weeks between terms. Mrs. Lumley knows Scotland fairly well, so they've decided to carry the torch of theatrical tradition — that's what she calls it — up and down the Caledonian Canal. I thought I'd join them and try to dig out some information about my pirate ancestor at the same time. Though I've warned them I'm likely to be whisked off at a moment's notice. They've managed to get the Globe — that's the caravan — as far as Fort William and I'm joining them there."

" Oh, fine! " cried Holly. " Perhaps we'll be able to see you."

" Are you staying there too? " Ross said.

" No. Daddy's school broke up before mine and they've gone on. We've got a sort of shack on an island called Fluran. It's way out beyond Mull. Daddy's writing its life history and Mother's painting its portrait. They're doing a book between them called *Fluran — Its Flora and Fauna* or something. If I know anything about Daddy, his boys are going to be jolly sick of Fluran and its bugs by the end of next term. Let's go back, shall we? I've got some food left in my box."

Between them, they demolished the seed cake and half the bottle of fizz Miss Charlotte had viewed with such disapproval.

The two elderly ladies had at last put away their books and were now snoring gently, wrapped in their blankets like two gray cocoons.

At last, Holly gave a great yawn and thumped the railway pillow.

" I'll be glad when we reach the border," she remarked. " It'll be cooler. Probably raining as well. People thought I was mad at King's Cross with this coat on. But I've been caught out by Scotland before. Now tell me all about the Navigation School," she added, settling down with her hands behind her head. " Did you have to do everything at the double? "

Ross stretched himself out on the opposite bunk.

" Cadets," he said in a heavy voice, " are treated as young men and " — he cleared his throat importantly — " are expected to behave as such. That's our signals instructor."

" Boats? " asked Holly drowsily.

" A hundred-ton training ketch, couple of whalers, motor launch, and so on. What's yours like? "

There was no reply.

Ross raised himself on his elbow and glanced across at Holly. She was fast asleep, her fair hair flung across the pillow. He leaned over and gently pulled the blanket up over her and a couple of minutes later was fast asleep himself.

The seven fifteen from King's Cross streamed on through the night, thundering toward the Scottish border.

2

THE GLOBE AND ATLAS

ALTHOUGH the sky was clear except for a few white balls of cloud, the vast hump of Ben Nevis cast a deep shadow over Fort William as the train ambled into the station.

Holly was hanging out of the window, examining the people on the platform. Ross had his head poked out too in the small space that was left. He was staring silently up at the mountain, so near it seemed to overhang Fort William like a brooding animal.

Holly glanced up at the Ben as the train hissed to a stop.

" When you're the other side of the Loch by the ferry, it looks just like a hippopotamus sitting down and sulking," she said, flinging open the door and gazing up and down the platform.

" Aunt Lottie was right," she said in a disgusted voice. " He's forgotten. Or run out of oil. I shall have to swim."

" Don't give up yet," Ross grinned, heaving down the kit. " Perhaps he's at the barrier."

" No," said Holly. " If he'd come, he'd have been on the platform. To collect the train numbers for Robert. He's my young brother. Did you notice the name of the engine that got us to Edinburgh, before they took off the Fort William coaches? Robert's an awful pest. It's the first thing he'll ask me."

" Mallard," said Ross.

" Are you a train fiend too? " laughed Holly.

" Not now," he admitted. " But you get into the habit of noticing things after a couple of terms at Navigation. Look! There's the Commander beating down on us."

A tall woman like the figurehead of a three-masted bark under full canvas came sailing along the platform, followed by a small man trotting along with a length of timber on his shoulder.

" Ah, dear boy! " boomed Mrs. Lumley. " So glad to see you're not afloat yet. Bumble, put that wood down."

Major Lumley dropped the ends of timber onto the platform and leaned against them, panting.

" How d'you do, Major," said Ross. " Where's Pud? "

" My niece is washing the theatrical costumes in Loch Linnhe. She's very extravagant with the soap, poor child, but perhaps it's the salt water. Bumble, remind me to get some more soap after breakfast. We waited breakfast. Is this young lady with you? " she added, bending a majestic look upon Holly.

Ross grinned and made hasty introductions. " No one's turned up to meet her," he said.

Mrs. Lumley's hand was warm and firm in Holly's.

" She shall breakfast with us. We've parked up by the old military road near a farmhouse. It's only a ten minutes' walk. Pick up the wood, Bumble, and give a hand with the suitcases."

Turning away, she sailed in front of them up the platform and through the barrier at such a pace that they had a job to keep up with her. Major Lumley and his timber immediately became involved with a bus that was turning out of the station.

Holly grinned delightedly at the fluent Scots of the bus driver and glanced behind her at the empty pier and slipway.

" I'd better leave a message at the Claymore where we always stay, in case Daddy turns up," she said.

In less than ten minutes they were cutting across the outskirts of Fort William toward the wild open country of the Lairigmore.

" Who's this Pud? " whispered Holly.

" Her real name's Pauline. We call her Pud or Spotted Dick because she's fat and freckled. Good sort, though. Mrs. Lumley's the commanding officer and poor old Pud's all the privates, eh, Major? " said Ross, giving him a hand with the other end of the timber.

Major Lumley sucked his mustache. " My wife's a wonderful woman. A woman of many parts. She says she'd be blunting the fine edge of her genius if she wasted her talents on anything less than top-level stuff."

Ross laughed. " I can just hear her saying it too! Hey, mind out! What's all the wood for? " he cried, as the wind caught Major Lumley and swung him around. " You ought to have a red flag on it! "

" My wife's designed a collapsible proscenium arch. Where the curtains hang, you know, and the lights are fixed," the Major said to Holly. " If you've got any curtains or lights, that is. Her idea is that it'll save painting a back cloth when we do open-air shows. The audience can just look through at the scenery wherever we happen to be."

" What's going to happen if it's an indoor scene? " inquired Ross.

The Major glanced severely at him. " My wife says that

Shakespeare didn't use scenery and what's good enough for Shakespeare, she'll make do with too," he said. "There's Pud! Wave to her for me, will you? "

A short dumpy girl with two plaits twisted on the top of her head was staggering up the slope toward them, carrying a laundry basket full of wet clothes.

" Hey, Pud! " Ross shouted. " Put it on your head and go all Eastern! It's simple that way. Can you manage the wood now, Major? I'll give poor old Pud a hand."

He dropped his end of the wood. Major Lumley sank to his knees, slowly righted himself and tottered on.

Ross caught hold of the basket. " Here, Pud, you take my kit bag. It's lighter than this washing. How much soap did you use on it after all? "

" Six bars," said Pud. Her plain kind face beamed with pleasure as she looked at Holly. " Hullo," she said.

" Hullo," smiled Holly. " Look, I'll take both cases. You look awfully hot."

" I am rather," Pud admitted. " It's all uphill from the Loch. It was lovely and cold in the water, though. Henry the Eighth's tunic floated away, and I had to go in after it. You're very pretty. Are you going to take the leads? "

" The leads? " said Holly.

" You know, the leading parts. Aunt Caroline isn't sure if Gina — that's my cousin — can come this time. She's waiting for a letter. Gina usually takes the romantic bits. I do the parts you don't have to be pretty for, like maids and page boys and things. And the stage-managing, of course. . . . Putting the chairs and tables where they're wanted in the play and pulling the curtains to and fro and telling people the words when they forget their parts and washing the costumes. You know, all the little jobs."

" Pud's too modest," called Ross. " She's just about the

hardest worker I know. Apart from our signals officer. And me, of course."

"If both my hands weren't full, I'd throw something," retorted Holly, laughing. "Conceited thing. Catch up a lump of grass, Pud, and aim for his head."

"I daren't," grinned Pud. "He can run a lot faster than I can!"

"Here we are. Welcome to the Globe," gasped Major Lumley, dropping the wood with a sigh of relief and wiping his face.

At the end of the slope stood a whitewashed farmhouse and at the back of it an old caravan badly in need of a coat of paint. The pleasant smell of bacon and eggs drifted from a drainpipe stuck through the roof.

"How perfectly darling!" cried Holly, as she stared at the faded sun canopies fixed over the windows. "It looks like a dear old cart horse in blinkers."

Major Lumley glanced at her anxiously.

"My wife's very attached to the Globe," he whispered.

"I was afraid it would be one of those streamlined things, all chromium and plate glass," said Holly. "This is a real gypsy one, except it's got a car instead of a horse."

"Atlas is a genuine 1902 model. Do you reckon she'll cope with these mountain roads?" said Ross, glancing affectionately at the car standing at the front. Mrs. Lumley appeared at the door of the Globe, holding a frying pan.

"Twenty years out, dear boy," she said. "Nineteen thirty-two. Been across the Sahara twice. It'll eat up these little Scottish hills. Bumble, bang two pieces of that wood into the ground. And fasten the towrope between them. Pud can hang up the washing."

"I thought the timber was for a proscenium arch, my dear," returned the Major mildly.

" So it is," replied Mrs. Lumley, producing a tablecloth which she laid on the ground. " A collapsible proscenium arch. When it's collapsed, it'll have a variety of other uses. Have your breakfast."

They all sat down on the ground around the tablecloth. As the Major had remarked earlier, the Commander was indeed a woman of many parts, one of them being that of an excellent cook. It wasn't long before she had piled the cloth with plates of smooth creamy porridge, a huge meat dish of bacon and eggs, plates of fried bread and toast, and a jar full of marmalade.

For a time there was complete silence, except for the crackle of toast and the munching of jaws.

Holly felt a thrill of excitement running through her as she breathed the cool flowing air off Loch Linnhe, scented with heather and wild flowers, and looked across at the hills of Druim Fada far off beyond Loch Eil, with the blue cloud shadows flowing over their green and gray.

She turned her eyes toward Loch Linnhe lying calm and blue below. " There's a launch or some sort of craft coming up from Corran Narrows," she said, screwing up her eyes. " If it's Daddy in *Sea Rider,* he's got it going full out. It's too far away to see yet."

The meat dish and the plates were soon empty. Ross scraped the last morsel of marmalade out of the jar and tried to make it cover the last piece of toast.

" To work! " announced Mrs. Lumley, rising majestically to her feet. " Fetch the bowl, Pud. Holly and Ross can wash up. You can tidy the Globe. Bumble, you get started on that clothesline. I'm going to type out some parts. Remember that the Globe Players open their summer season in a week's time. The glorious torch of theatrical tradition must be upheld worthily by the Globe Players!

Into the breach, dear friends! Bumble, don't stand there staring. Go and find the hammer."

She disappeared into the caravan. A moment later the clack-clack of the typewriter came spurting out of the open door like machine-gun fire.

Ross, with the Commander's apron around his waist, directed his attention to the serious job of washing up. Holly watched his face, with its firm lips and serious eyes. I'm going to like him more than I've ever liked anyone before in my life, she thought. He goes about a horrid job like washing up just the same as he would if he were reefing a mainsail or bringing a ship up a narrow channel.

" Hey, wake up! " Ross grinned suddenly. " This pile of plates is going over backward if you don't do something about it! "

Just after midday, when the theatrical washing was drying on the towrope, they were all once more sitting around the tablecloth in the center of which stood an enamel teapot and a plate of chocolate biscuits. They were waiting to start the first rehearsal. The Commander, in a final frenzy of machine-gun fire, was typing the last of the parts.

Holly watched the mounting flight of a meadow pipit as it rose faster and faster against the distant hills until, planing suddenly down again, it alighted with a clicking, whirring twitter on the roof of the caravan. Ross sat down beside her and began pouring out the tea.

" How ever d'you manage? " Holly said to Pud, with her mouth full of chocolate biscuit. " There are only four of you, five when Gina comes. Are there any plays with only five people in them? The ones we did at school seemed to have dozens of parts. To get as many people in as possible, I suppose, though they all seemed terribly dull, mostly Cranford and lumps of Shakespeare with all the rude bits cut out, worse luck."

Pud grinned and tried to tuck her sturdy legs into an imitation of Holly's easy cross-legged position on the grass.

" Sometimes we do things that only need a couple of players and Aunt Caroline's got a whole heap of sketches she does on her own. She plans to end the tour with acting some of the old Scottish legends in the open. That's what the new arch is for. Quick, Ross! Stop Henry the Eighth's pants! They've blown off the line again. Now my maid's apron's gone. Do hurry, Ross. They'll be at the bottom of the slope by now and I'll have to start washing all over again! "

Ross only settled himself more comfortably on the grass. Holly leaped up, vaulted over the tablecloth, aimed a hearty kick at Ross in passing, and caught up with the runaway laundry which was lying spread out across the old military road.

" Gosh! " groaned Pud. " I do wish we had some pegs." She picked up the potato peeler and began on the bowl of potatoes in front of her.

" But what happens if you get a play with an old woman or something like that in it? " resumed Holly, sitting down to recover her breath. " The Commander couldn't take an old part, could she? "

" That's what you think! " Pud retorted. " She's absolutely marvelous. She seems to shrink to half her size, her hands go all shaky, and even her voice is different."

Holly glanced warily at Ross, who was staring across at the distant hills lost in thought.

" But her face! " she objected, seizing the opportunity to poke a piece of prickly grass down the back of his collar.

" Haven't you ever heard of make-up? " laughed Pud.

" A base of Number Five — that's a yellowy-pink color — and some white and black liner — that's a stick like a pencil — and a bit of crimson lake and you couldn't tell her from seventy or eighty. At a distance, of course. Though it's not as easy as it sounds. I'll show you the make-up box later. I can do a bit, but you have to be pretty clever to put it on properly and know all about the face bones and muscles under the skin and how all sorts of faces go when they get old."

" Miss Bromley wouldn't let us use make-up in our plays, silly old fossil. Where ignorance is bliss! Nearly all the girls in the sixth wear make-up on week ends. She'd pass out if she knew."

Ross reached silently behind him while Holly was speaking, caught hold of her wrist and she found herself rolling down the slope. She picked herself up, caught hold of a clump of damp earth and flung it. The clump hit the Commander fair and square on the chin as she emerged from the Globe and sent the typewritten parts flying out of her hand, where they were taken up by the wind and tossed in all directions.

Holly gasped and bit her lip.

" Bad shot," said the Commander calmly, brushing the worst of the mud off the front of her blouse. " See if you can catch them, dear child, before they blow to Inverness. I like to keep the program a surprise if possible."

Holly raced toward the nearest sheet of paper and put her foot on it. Pud caught up the potato peeler and speared the rest.

" That'll teach you not to poke grass down the necks of jujitsu fiends," whispered Ross, his amber eyes flashing with amusement. " Compulsory course, School of Navigation."

" Just you wait. You'll get it back," muttered Holly, grinning.

" Come along, boys and girls," announced Mrs. Lumley brightly. " Let us press on. Let us resolve to make this the best show we boys and girls have ever put on, shall we? That includes you, Bumble," she added. " Do wake up and try to concentrate. We're starting with one of our Victorian blood-and-thunders. I shall want you with a Devon dialect, so start brushing it up. Holly can read Gina's part. I'll just fill up the teapot and then we'll really get cracking. Give out the parts, Pud."

Pud pulled the sheets off the potato peeler and handed them around.

" Listen! " said Holly, suddenly. " Can you hear the pipes somewhere? "

From the distance toward Loch Linnhe the plaintive sound drifted toward them on the wind.

" Getting ready for the Highland Games, I expect. I'd love to see a sword dance done really well," she sighed.

" What's a sword dance? " said Ross, flipping over the pages of his part.

Holly jumped up. She picked up the potato peeler and laid it on a flat piece of grass. " This is a sword. Now I want another. That stick'll do. You lay them down across each other." Kicking off her shoes, she whirled into a riotous dance, stepping in and out between the potato peeler and the stick, with flying kilt and tossing hair.

" We need some music," she gasped.

" Sing then," suggested Pud. " We'll join in and clap for you."

The Commander, just about to put the lid on the teapot, froze into stillness at the sound of a powerful young voice singing " The Hundred Pipers " outside.

As it dissolved into a gale of laughter, she stepped from the door and confronted Holly.

" Where did you get that voice? " she demanded.

" Sorry," mumbled Holly, " I — I was only showing them a sword dance."

" Don't be sorry, dear child! Be proud. One day we shall remember we heard that voice for the first time by the waters of Lock Linnhe."

" Do sing something else," begged Pud. " Just one."

She stared up at Holly, who raised her eyes to the blue of the distant summits and sang the " Road to the Isles," her clear, sweet voice joining the song of the skylarks over the grassy hillocks.

They were all silent when she ended.

" It's just as if the mountains were singing," Pud said, wiping her eyes.

" H'm," said Mrs. Lumley, gazing thoughtfully at Holly. " What a pity Gina's coming! "

Ross said nothing. His face was pale under its tan.

" What's the matter, Ross? " Holly said, sitting down beside him. He shook himself suddenly and smiled. " Nothing. Only when you were singing that about ' It's the blue islands from the Skerries to the Lews,' I had such a strange feeling. Just as if I wanted to remember something and couldn't. Hullo! Who's this dashing up the slope? "

Holly shielded her eyes with her hand. " It's Andy from the Claymore. That must have been *Sea Rider* coming up Loch Linnhe after all. Hi, Andy! Don't kill yourself! "

Andy's thin legs flashed to a halt. He threw back his tousled mop of ginger hair.

" Your faither, Miss Holly, and your mither. And wee Robert. Waitin' for ye."

" Waiting for me! I like that! " Holly retorted. " It's me

that's been waiting for them! Where are they? "

" Th' guidman's haein' his parritch and Mistress Gordon's a wee a-back th' pier. Th' bairn's awa' tae th' station."

" Daddy eating porridge at this hour! It's nearly dinner time! "

" He sayd he canna dae withouten his breakfas'. He's haein' his breakfas' an' his dinner taegither. An' he sayd ye're not tae dander but tae come belive."

" In other words, I've got to look sharp," Holly grinned. " Give me a hand with my case, will you, Andy? "

" Aye, I'll gie a lift," said Andy, eying the biscuits.

" We'll all go and give you a send-off," announced the Commander. " Though I'm sure I wish you weren't going. Remind me about the soap, Pud. And some more Wet White for the make-up box. And needles for the sewing machine. I know I shall want to run up some costumes for our Scottish legends program. Bumble, get up and brush that grass off yourself. We're going to meet Holly's people. We don't want them to think we're a lot of tramps. Which they will if they see you like that with half the Ben Nevis foothills in your hair."

3

A GORDON! A GORDON!

HOLLY, with her retinue of Globe Players, re-entered Fort William High Street in state, with Andy as outrider licking the coating off a chocolate biscuit.

The Commander had put on a large black hat and cloak which flapped and flowed in the breeze off the Loch and caused a sensation among a party of Norwegian climbers setting out for Ben Nevis.

They had crossed the Square and come in sight of the landing stage when she suddenly let out a shout and pounded down toward the slipway. " A Gordon! A Gordon! " yelled Holly.

The war cry of the Gordons answered her. The Globe Players saw her caught by a tall man and kissed energetically. Holly began dragging him toward the group. And then she dropped him and flew to the slipway.

" Mother! Come down to earth for a minute. I've got some wonderful people to show you."

The woman who walked lightly up the steps was a small slender copy of the vigorous Holly, with smooth fair hair coiled on her neck and large butterfly-blue eyes. She tossed her sketchbook back into *Sea Rider* and looked up at her daughter.

" Really, Holly," she said quietly, " you are an extremely noisy person! I thought the town was being invaded."

Holly smiled and bit her lip and, catching Leonie Gordon by the hand, pulled her toward the Globe Players.

The Commander, standing calm and majestic in their midst, looked hard at Mrs. Gordon, who stopped and stared back.

" Little Leonardo! " cried the Commander.

" Why, Jumbo! " cried Leonie Gordon in turn and flew toward the Commander's outstretched hand.

" Is it possible, Leonardo, that you are actually the mother of that enormous child? " demanded Mrs. Lumley. " You haven't changed a bit. Except, of course, you've given up wearing a gym slip."

" I'm thirty-seven now, Jumbo," confessed Mrs. Gordon.

The Commander paused and looked uncomfortable.

" I would prefer you to forget that somewhat unfortunate nickname," she said heavily. " It might — undermine the dignity of my theatrical work. Leonardo is a different matter. I shall continue to call you Leonardo."

She turned to Holly. " We sixth-formers called her that after the great Da Vinci. She was a bit of a genius even when she was your age in the junior art class."

The Commander gazed down from her great height at the slender Leonie Gordon with something like humility in her eyes.

They had by now become the center of an interested group, which included not only the rest of the Globe Players and Charles Gordon but a good proportion of the passengers at the coach station. The Commander looked round, dismissed the bus passengers with a regal nod, and said, " Coffee all around on me."

Andy, with a sharp eye for the continued prosperity of

the Claymore, led them into the dining room and disappeared with instructions to get Robert out of the station and return him without delay, as the tide was on the turn.

Robert, short, square, and with a rebellious lower lip, appeared on the slipway as they were loading *Sea Rider* with stores. He stood with his hands behind his back and his stomach stuck out, glaring down at Holly.

" A Gordon, A Gordon," he remarked grudingly.

" A Gordon, A Gordon," said Holly.

They eyed each other warily.

" Bet you forgot," went on Robert with gloomy satisfaction.

" Mallard," said Holly.

Robert's face lighted up suddenly into sweetness.

" I've brought you a present," he said, turning out his pockets onto the slipway. " It's a funny long empty stone."

He separated the stone from some plasticine and bus tickets and tossed it down to Holly, who was stowing the wooden cases in *Sea Rider*'s cabin.

" It's only an ordinary stone, dear," said Holly.

" But it's empty! " protested Robert. " No stone was ever empty before."

" Thanks very much all the same," replied Holly, putting it into the pocket of her duffle coat. " Oh, Daddy," she wailed, " couldn't we have baked beans for a change? This case says it's got fifty tins of spaghetti in it! "

" Spaghetti's a halfpenny cheaper than baked beans," remarked the Commander severely. She had discarded the black cloak and hat and was actually taking part in the chain of hands passing the store cases from the landing stage down the slipway.

Holly looked up from the cabin to where Ross in shirt sleeves was laughing with Pud on the slip. She watched his eyes flashing with merriment at something Pud had said and felt a pang of regret at having to leave the Globe Players.

Ross caught her eye and swung down the steps and into *Sea Rider* with the ease of a practiced seaman.

"That's the last box in," he said. "You've got a bit of everything now. Though when you arrive, I expect you'll find you've forgotten something vital like the salt and pepper!"

Holly steadied herself against the roof of the cabin.

"Come in a minute and see if I've stowed away properly."

Ross bent his head and followed her inside to the crowded little cabin. The storm lantern on its hook moved gently to the swing of Loch Linnhe against the slipway.

"I wish I was coming with you," Ross said, folding his arms and staring from the porthole down at the water.

"And I wish I wasn't going," replied Holly. "No. I don't really mean that. I want to be away to the Islands and away with you too. You're going to have some fun."

Ross nodded. "We may come across each other again one of these days."

He picked up *The Hooded Horror Strikes Again* from where Holly had flung it on the bunk with her coat. "He looks a pretty first-class criminal."

"That's just the point!" Holly cried triumphantly. "Everyone thinks that, but he's really a detective in disguise! He's Scotland Yard's prize wizard and he gets into the most terrific jams. Aunt Lottie sneers at the Hooded Horror, but honestly I think he's educational and I've told her so, but she can't see it."

Ross grinned. "That's an idea!" he exclaimed. "You do a bit of detective work and find out all about my pirate ancestor for me."

Holly's eyes brightened but became thoughtful again.

" But I haven't a single clue! " she said. " Can't you give me any leads at all? Some scrap of information to begin working on? Didn't your father ever say anything about him? "

" I don't think he knew much except that his name was Ross and he was a pirate–smuggler–cattle-thief somewhere in seventeen eighty something."

Sea Rider lurched as Charles Gordon jumped down and began to crank the engine. Ross got to his feet and held out his hand.

" This seems like good-by for the time being," he said. " Don't forget to dig me up a good heap of treasure as well! I think I'd like it to be in a cave — yes, definitely a cave."

Holly laughed. " Silly! Those things only happen in books out of the children's library! You never get caves and treasure in real life. But I might be able to put the bits I know together and shake them up and see what comes out. Where'll I send letters? "

" Fort William this week," replied Ross. " Inverkenneth next week, then Fort Augustus the week after, and last week Inverness. Write care of the post office. We finish after that back at Fort William with the Commander's Scottish legends program. It lasts only about an hour but it's going to be awfully good. I've got to be the Highland chieftain, she says, in full war paint."

" That reminds me," Holly groaned. " I don't even know what clan you belong to. What a hope! Trying to build you a family tree out of nothing."

Sea Rider began vibrating as Charles Gordon started up the engine. Ross left the cabin and leaped to the slipway.

" If you find anything out or think of anything you've forgotten to tell me, send a wire," called Holly.

Ross grimaced down at her.

" I really mean it," she added. " Fluran's got a telephone. Just been put in. The number's Fluran One. It's no good asking for Two, Three, or Four, because there aren't any! Just One and aren't they proud of it! Daddy says everyone on the island downs tools when a call comes through."

" Fluran One. It doesn't sound too difficult to remember," Ross laughed. He helped Leonie Gordon down into the well of the boat and steadied Robert. Charles Gordon cast off the rope.

" Good-by, Mrs. Lumley. Good-by, Major," called Holly. " I'll send you a wire for your opening night. 'By, Pud. Give my love to the theatrical costumes and don't forget to buy some pegs! "

Sea Rider was gliding off from the slip when Ross gave a startled shout and clapped his hand to his pocket.

" Hey, Holly! " he yelled. " I've thought of a clue. Coming over! For Pete's sake don't drop it in the water. It belonged to the Old Villain himself. Been handed down. All that remains of family inheritance! "

Holly leaned out over the gunwale. Ross tossed a small object into her outstretched hands.

" Well held! " he called. " Keep it safe. It was the Old Villain's snuffbox."

Sea Rider swung away and headed down Loch Linnhe.

" When's dinner? " asked Holly.

" No more food until we reach Fluran," Charles Gordon grinned.

" But I haven't eaten since breakfast! All of you stoked up in Fort William! " Holly exploded wrathfully.

Leonie Gordon laughed at the sight of her disgusted face. " Cheer up, darling. He's only teasing. We know quite

well how often you have to restoke! There's a piece of wood loose in the spaghetti box. Get out a tin and heat it on the primus. The loaf's in that biscuit tin under the table."

Holly, too hungry to grumble about spaghetti, emptied three tins into the saucepan, cut the loaf in half, and climbed out onto the cabin roof.

They were running past the white lighthouse on Corran Ferry and rocking in the wash of a cargo vessel. Holly held her plate steady and, with her mouth full, pointed dumbly at the boat.

" Probably bauxite for the works at Fort William," her father remarked. " They unload at that pier above ours."

Holly swallowed another mouthful. "What's bauxite? It sounds heathenish."

" Nothing more alarming than aluminum oxide, if you want to be technical. It's a precious ore and the only source of aluminum. That lot's been dug out of Spain or France, I expect."

" Isn't there any in Scotland? " Holly said, idly watching the vessel plowing on toward Fort William.

" A little and even that's worth its weight in gold." He eased the tiller and *Sea Rider* began to swing around the point and out into the wider waters of the Sea Loch.

" I like your Ross," Leonie remarked. " He has the most paintable face. I don't think I've ever met anyone with stranger eyes. Almost a golden color. They light up in the most peculiar way at times."

" He's got a strange great-great-grandfather too," replied Holly. " He's given me the job of finding out all about him. I suppose he thinks I'd be good at the detective business," she added modestly.

Charles Gordon grinned. " Got any clues? "

" Only this," and Holly handed him the snuffbox.

" H'm," her father said thoughtfully, when he had examined it closely. " Rounded and black with a homemade hinged lid that is scratched on the top and underneath. Wait a minute! I wonder whether they are scratches. Or letters."

" Daddy! " gulped Holly.

" Don't get excited. You'll have to wait until we get to Fluran and I can have another look through my magnifying glass."

" You've got another clue as well," Leonie put in. " The ancestor was a Celt."

" H-how do you know? " Holly stammered.

" By Ross's coloring. Pure auburn hair, light eyes, fair skin under that tan, powerful build . . ."

" Which means his forebears came from somewhere north of the Highland Line, if he is a Celt," put in her father. " I remember that distinctly from Bastable Minor's essay on Early Racial Distribution. He made a most unpleasant hash of the spelling."

Holly's face glowed. " I'm getting on, aren't I? It's marvelous what you can find out if you use your brains."

" Whose brains? " her father inquired dryly. " All you've got to do now is to find the exact spot north of the Highland Line."

" Y-es. That's all," said Holly.

4

FLURAN ONE

THE next morning after breakfast, Holly lay sprawled among a mass of wild flowers, pretending to watch the sea moving under a light wind which tossed great wafts of clover scent over Fluran. Actually she had one eye on her father, who sat beside her examining the snuffbox through his glass.

" Done it yet, Daddy? " she said for the fifth time.

" Almost," he replied absently. " The letters are Gaelic and they go around in two circles on the inside of the lid, with an E — I think it's an E — right in the middle."

" Gaelic? " Holly whistled in dismay. " Who's going to be able to translate that for me? "

" Shouldn't be too difficult. Iain might know, or Miss Ethnie at the post office. Most of the older people have a little of the Gaelic. Here you are! "

He handed her his notebook in which he had written.

" THA SLUAGH GAM' CHUAIRTEACHADH ACH THA MI NAM AONAR."

Holly rolled her eyes despairingly. " What a ghastly mouthful! "

Her father grinned. " Don't start giving up yet! Run over to the ferry and see if you can find Iain."

Holly got up and shook the grass from her hair. " Have you seen Jamie yet, Daddy? I was wondering if he still has that lovely pigeon."

" He was up a couple of days ago with a load of peats for the fire, with Annie riding on his shoulder. She's fatter than ever. You'll probably see him on the slipway."

Holly set off up Cairnmor, with its loose stones giving way as she climbed higher to great drifts of purple moor grass and heather. The mail boat was just being pulled in down below when she reached the top. Every inhabitant on the island, it seemed, had come to welcome the mails and make a bid to be the first to snatch the newspapers ashore. Holly raced down the long slope to the causeway.

" Hi! Iain! Remember me? " she called to a tall, old man with the mailbag. His weather-beaten face creased into a smile and at once resumed its ferocious expression.

" Awa' back wi' ye." He spoke with authority to the crowd. " Dinna ye rush Her Britannic Majesty's mails! Awa', ye haverels " and he stamped his boots and thrust at the throng with his stick.

" 'Tis th' great minnit o' their day," he confided to Holly. " There's naething for them tae be thinkin' aboot an' th' mails gaes tae their heids." He received the package tossed to him from the boat and gravely strapped it into his post bag.

" Why do you trouble to do it all up? " Holly smiled. " The post office is only about two steps away."

Iain regarded her sternly. " 'Tis dangerous worrk. I dinna wish tae be murdered by this mob fashin' for their letters. I hae tae sort it firrst."

" Well, if there's one for us, I'll take it," Holly said.

" I ken well whaur ye are," Iain answered severely. " Ye'll dae nae such thing. 'Tis agley th' regulations for

unauthorized perrsons tae handle th' mails! "

" But it'll save you a long walk," Holly protested.

" 'Tis paid I am for th' lang walk," replied Iain, tossing the mailbag over his shoulder.

" Well then," went on Holly, " do you know anyone who has the Gaelic? I want something translated into English."

Iain pursed his lips. " There'll be auld Niall th' shepherd awa' up on Drumsallie."

" But he won't be able to read, will he? " asked Holly.

" Indade and he wull! " put in Iain indignantly. " They a' hae th' good education in th' islands. Niall too wull be daein' th' beautiful clear handwriting! "

Holly looked suitably downcast at the insult she had offered the shepherd. Iain allowed a smile to lighten his face.

" This'll be th' road," he said, pointing toward a ridge on the other side of Cairnmor. " Ye canna miss Niall."

Holly found the old man sitting outside his hut with a pretty black dog at his feet. He listened silently to her story. " Show me thy paper, lass," he said at last.

She handed him her father's notebook. He stared for a long time at the Gaelic and then turned his eyes toward the moor. " Aye," he said. " May be th' clan watchworrd o' a muckle swankie. O' a proud mon an' an independent that would owe naught tae his neighbor. Yet may be lonely in his pride. Ye can tak' it as ' Alone, though surrounded ' in the English."

Holly looked up at him. " I still don't really know what it means," she smiled. " How can you be alone if you are surrounded? And surrounded by what? "

Niall spread out his hands. " Th' auld watchworrds be like th' moor. Muckle drear and empty fra th' distance but fu' of blossoms and beasties when fowk come close." He smiled. "A mon can be alone when he is surrounded by his enemies, lassie. Or maybe 'tis like th' wee island there." He pointed across the sea to where Iona lay small and low like a lamb at the foot of the towering red cliffs of Mull. "She is a wee drap o' land alone in th' sea wi' th' great waters all round her."

Holly nodded thoughtfully and thanked him. She walked slowly back over the ridge of Drumsallie and looked down at the ferry. The inhabitants were once more running toward the post office. No ship was in sight. And anyway I know jolly well there's only one mail a day, she thought. It must be a fire. But no smoke drifted to the sky other than the usual trail from the peats.

A new thought struck her. Perhaps the post office had been robbed and Miss Ethnie banged on the head and unconscious.

Forgetting all about the watchword, she skated hastily down over the stones and tufts of grass, flew along the path, leaped the burn by the causeway, and joined the surging crowd on the landing place.

Flurried whispers beat around her as she pushed her way toward Miss Ethnie's cottage, which also served as the post office. Faces were raised to the sky, necks craned out watching the thin line of Argyll mainland. Perhaps it's an aircraft, Holly thought, craning her neck with the rest. And then she caught sight of Jamie with his pigeon Annie on his shoulder. Annie regarded Holly with a cold, round, calculating eye as Jamie turned to grin at her.

"What's going on?" Holly gasped. "What's coming? Is it a plane?"

Jamie grimaced in disgust. "Planes is nowt to us. We sees 'em all th' time gaein' frae Tiree tae Glasgow an' back." His voice dropped. " Nay, 'tis a — telegram, comin' ower th' watter frae Fort William! Wi' nae wires! 'Twill drap frae th' sky intae post office. Such rare thing never happened afore, not sin' auld Willy Reekie swam tae Mull an' back wi' nae claes on."

Holly longed to hear about the exploits of Willy Reekie. But she tried to look as if she wanted to buy a stamp and fought her way to the post office. The little postmistress sat on a chair, surrounded by beshawled women who were offering her sips of water.

" Dinna fash," said one. " We'll stand by ye when — when it comes on ye."

Holly dropped on her knees. " Do you remember me, Miss Ethnie? It's Holly Gordon. What ever's the matter? Are you ill? "

The same woman spoke again. " 'Tis th' nerves, puir crittur. She's put her lace telephone cap on that she keeps for when she haes tae use th' instrument but she's guid for naething the noo, I reckon. She's all of a twitter."

They glanced cautiously at the telephone, which stood on a shelf covered with a cloth.

" I'll take it for you," Holly said. " You needn't be frightened of it. It's only like an ordinary call. Who's the telegram for? "

" We dinna ken," gasped Miss Ethnie. " I can dae th' calls but telegrams is richt fearful."

" There's no difference whatever," repeated Holly firmly. " But I'll take it for you and you can pass it on to the person it belongs to. There's the bell."

She lifted the receiver, pulled the notebook and pencil from her pocket, and began to write down the message. And then suddenly she clapped her hand over the receiver. " It's for my mother, Miss Ethnie," she whispered.

"DEAREST LEONARDO," went the telegram, "CAN HOLLY COME JOIN GLOBE PLAYERS STOP GINA GONE FRUIT PICKING KENT STOP THE NINNY STOP IF SHE CAN MAKE OBAN ROSS FETCH HER FROM THERE STOP DONT SAY NO STOP LIFE AND DEATH STOP WIRE YES TO CLAYMORE JUMBO."

"Wow!" yelled Holly, slamming down the receiver and flinging her arms around Miss Ethnie, who promptly fainted. "Just let me get over Cairnmor and back and you'll have another telegram to deal with."

Directly she reached home Holly poured out the news that she was about to enter the theatrical profession.

"Oh?" said Leonie casually, mashing up some more potatoes. "To whom was the wire addressed?"

Holly's face fell. She blushed and bit her lip. "For you, Mother," she said in a small voice.

Leonie smiled. "All right, you may go if we can think of a way of getting you to Oban. Caroline will see you behave yourself."

Holly's vitality returned with amazing speed. "The water's very calm," she remarked idly.

Charles Gordon burst out laughing. "You may take the boat if you want to. I think I can trust a Sea Ranger. Run over and send your wire. You can be off by half past three if you hurry up."

Darkness was falling as Holly headed around the Point of Kerrera and up into the Sound. The waters of Oban Bay, sprinkled with the riding lights of countless yachts, needed concentrated seamanship. She breathed a sigh of relief as she switched to dead slow and clutched at a mooring ring in the wall.

The slight impact brought *Sea Rider*'s bow perilously close to the stern of a blue and white luxury launch blazing with electricity and chromium plate and vibrating to the thump of feet and a noisy radio.

Then Holly caught sight of Ross standing with his arms folded farther along the wall, glaring down at the launch with an expression of disgust on his face.

" Ahoy there, landlubber! " she shouted. Her voice was drowned by the blare next door. She dashed into the cabin, snapped open her case, and felt for her Sea Ranger call.

The thin shrill wail of the bosun's pipe rose clear of the dance music. She saw Ross drop his arms. He glanced rapidly up and down the craft and saw her fair head shining in the lights from the launch.

" Reporting for duty, ma'am," he said, saluting.

" Stand easy! " ordered Holly. " Oh, Ross, it is good to see you again! How's everyone? "

" Good-oh," Ross said. " The Commander's bought some green paint and gone into the decorating business. We're jazzing up the Globe."

" And the Major? " asked Holly.

" He got more paint in his hair than on the woodwork, so that Commander's put him onto turning the handle of the sewing machine. She's making new sun canopies. The Major's awfully sick. About turning the handle, I mean."

" How did you get here? " Holly asked.

" Hopped onto the two o'clock steamer from Fort William."

" You must have practically flown to have caught the two o'clock. I didn't ring up the Claymore until half past one."

" Andy's got long legs." Ross grinned. " He came tearing in and I went tearing out! I got a single on the boat. I guessed you'd bring *Sea Rider.*"

" Oh, good," Holly cried. " Then we can take *Sea Rider* up to Fort William. Daddy said I was to leave it at Oban if you couldn't come with me because of those tricky islands around Lismore. And that reminds me. Ross, I'm practically the greatest detective in the world. The Hooded Horror's just a poor boob of an amateur." And she told him the results of her investigations.

" So you're pretty certain the Old Villain was a Highlander," he said slowly.

" And that makes you a Highlander too, remember," Holly pointed out. " First thing in the morning I'm going to start my case file on Ross Mordley. I shall want a nice big exercise book. Who knows? You may be the long-lost heir to vast estates! "

" Now who's been to the children's library? " Ross grinned. " I say, I think I'd better phone a message back to the Claymore to say we're coming up in *Sea Rider*. Andy'll run up with it if he's not in bed."

In less than ten minutes Ross had dropped once more into the boat.

" We ought to get started. It's going to take us a good time with the tide against us."

" I'm ready," Holly said. " You take over and I'll be the crew.

" Unship the mooring cable then," ordered Ross. " And don't get your sharp end mixed up with the monstrosity next door," he added sternly, jerking his thumb at the launch.

Holly choked, pulled the rope from the ring, and eased away from the wall.

The wind freshened as the mainland dropped behind and *Sea Rider* plowed toward the beam of Lismore Lighthouse.

" She's laboring a bit," Ross remarked, buttoning up the collar of his rainciat. " We're not making much headway. I've got her full out too."

" You won't get more than seven or eight knots out of *Sea Rider*. You've been spoiled by the vision of the superstreamlined, technicolor effort at Oban! "

" Did you notice the name? " grinned Ross. " The *Peek-a-Boo*."

" I don't believe you," exclaimed Holly. " Nobody could be so awful."

" Cross my heart. Painted in dainty foot-high letters as well. Though she was a lovely job. Just fallen in with bad company."

They were entering the Sea Loch and under the lee of Lismore.

" That's better," Ross exclaimed. " Now we can get a move on. How about a cup of really strong intoxicating cocoa? "

Pud was waiting for them as they tied up at the landing stage at Fort William.

" Oh, you are a sport! " Holly cried, looking up at the merry, freckled face. " It is nice to be met! How did you manage to wake up? "

" Put the scrubbing brush in my sleeping bag," Pud grinned. " And every time I turned over it woke me up to look at the time."

" Would you like some bacon? " Holly said. " I think there's a bit left."

" Don't use your bacon. Let's cook a fish," suggested Pud.

" Where do we get a fish from at this time of the morning? "

" Out of the water," Pud retorted. " I wasn't sure what time you'd be here, so I came down at four and had a snoop round. I — well, I borrowed a rowing boat and went fishing in the Loch."

" Honestly, Pud, you're marvelous," said Holly. " Catch anything? "

Pud had left her fishing tackle propped up against the coach station. " Here you are," she said. " They're not very big."

" Trout! " exclaimed Holly. " You have to be clever to catch trout. Beginner's luck, I expect."

The Globe presented a remarkably piebald appearance as they came up the slope. One half was still shabby. The other sparkled with fresh green in the morning sun. They crept about picking up the wood and trying not to wake the occupants of the Globe until breakfast was well under way.

" Get it hot," whispered Holly, " and then when it's glowing and the smoke's gone, we'll start the fish."

" Where's the grill? " asked Ross, arranging some stones round the fire.

Holly grimaced. " I hadn't thought of that."

" What about the piece of wire netting Aunt Caroline uses for props? " suggested Pud.

Luckily Atlas had been detached from the caravan and now stood some distance away, so they were able to lift out the wire netting.

" Whatever use can this be on a stage? " said Holly.

" Rocks," Pud said. " You scruggle the wire into a rough heap and drape a bit of sacking painted gray over it, tuck in the ends, and there you are! A jolly lifelike rock. Aunt Caroline uses a rock in the *Rain Song.*"

" What's that about? " Holly asked, laying the trout over the fire.

" It's an old fairy story about a mermaid who can't get back into the sea and she calls to the oyster catcher to help her."

" I know! " Holly cried. " The oyster catcher is supposed to be able to call the rain down. It's black and white with a long orange beak and says, ' Kleep Kleep,' and in twenty-four hours you get rain."

Pud nodded. " We've got a curtain of silver beads that we let down at the end and it looks just as if rain is falling while the mermaid sings the rain song. That was where Gina used to come unstuck. In the singing bit, I mean. I expect Aunt Caroline will cast you as the mermaid. You'll have a beautiful tail and long golden hair. Here! How did I get on to talking plays? "

" Wire netting and fish tails," Ross grinned. " And breakfast's burning."

" It is not," retorted Holly, touching the trout with her penknife. " Better give the Commander the ' wakee wakee.' "

" You do it," Ross said. " It's your bosun's pipe."

" Not me! " laughed Holly. " I don't know what she feels like first thing in the morning! "

" She's always the same," Pud said. " Calm and unruffled. You watch. She'll fling open the door of the Globe and sail down the steps as if she were going to take a triumphant curtain call! "

Pud was right. The Commander, beaming graciously, appeared at the door and contrived to make a Japanese kimono and curlers look imposing.

" Ah, boys and girls! So I've been let off the cooking! And Pud's been putting her father's teaching to good account! Bumble, wake up. We've got fish."

Ross saw Holly's puzzled look. "Ever heard of John Broome-Gilson, marine biologist and dry-fly fisherman?" he inquired.

"Not the man who wrote *British Sea Life*? Daddy's got it."

"John Broome-Gilson's her father," grinned Ross.

Holly went scarlet. "W-why didn't someone tell me?" she stammered. "I p-patted her on the head and acted all superior and told her she was having beginner's luck!"

"Why should it make any difference because I'm Pauline Broome-Gilson?" Pud demanded. "People should be liked for what they can do themselves, not because they've got clever fathers! Anyone can stick a line over the side of a boat. It's still luck if they catch anything."

"Well spoken, O wise and speckled steamed Pudding," said Ross, pulling one of her pigtails.

The Commander smiled dreamily. "We are a very gifted family. All except Pud's silly Aunt Dolly, who married that sillier man with the grocer's shop on the Moray Firth somewhere. I remember she looked like a horse and thought she could act. Bumble, wash up. Holly must come in with me and go over her parts. I can spare you a couple of hours, dear child."

The two hours extended into three of absorbing work for Holly, punctuated with the slap of Ross's brush on the outside of the Globe. It was nearly midday before they came out of rehearsal, their eyes dazzled by the sunshine and the smartness of the rejuvenated Globe.

"I am highly pleased," beamed the Commander. "She's going to be quite a credit to us when she's had some more practice."

Pud rushed up to Holly. "I knew you'd be good," she

cried. " Look! I've been to the shops."

She pressed a large, red exercise book into Holly's hands. " Is it what you wanted? "

" Pud, you're the purest saint! Let me pay. I've got ten shillings."

Pud shook her plaits vigorously. " No," she said. " It's a good-luck present. You can't buy good luck."

5

ON STAGE!

FRIDAY came all too soon for Holly. Now that the opening night of the Globe Players' summer season was actually upon her, she had a sinking feeling every time she thought of eight o'clock.

She was busy fixing the new green sun canopies over the windows and going through her part with Ross, who lay on his back underneath the caravan painting the inside of the wheels daffodil yellow.

" 'Be my bride or out into the storm with you,' " said Ross, running the brush carefully along one of the spokes.

" 'Never, sir!' " cried Holly. " 'No one shall buy my heart. I'll take my bundle and wander — wander through the world earning an honest crust rather than — rather than marry such a — monster as you.' Drat it, that's the third time I've hit my thumb. 'Oh, sir, be kind to my poor old parents!' "

Holly flung down the hammer. "It's no good, Ross. I can't do it. I'm dead scared."

"Of course you're scared and of course you can do it," retorted Ross. "You've got a touch of first-night jitters, that's all. Everybody who's any good gets them. Even Sir Laurence Olivier."

" How do you know? " exclaimed Holly. " And anyway I don't believe it."

Ross grinned good-humoredly at her through the wheel. " It's a fact. You ask the Commander. The greater the actor, the worse the jitters. She says no one who isn't nervous when the call boy shouts, ' Five minutes ' will ever give a great performance."

" Are you scared too? " said Holly.

" Frightened out of my wits," Ross admitted. " Come on, let's do it once more."

Holly picked up the hammer and moved the steps along to the next window. She could see Pud inside the caravan stitching green and blue sequins to some bare patches in the mermaid's tail. The Commander sat beside her separating the strands from a plait of blond theatrical hair and sewing them to a canvas skull cap.

" You're going to look a riot in this," called Pud, when she saw Holly's face at the window. " The producer wants you to wear a shell necklace."

" ' I'll have you, yea or nay,' " came Ross's voice, deep and foreboding from underneath the Globe. " ' I have a vast estate . . . a vast estate . . . a . . . vast estate . . .' "

" What! Not three vast estates, sir! " mocked Holly, jumping down. " Now who's forgetting the lines? "

The Commander came to the door and beckoned to her. " Just let me see how this fits, dear child. H'm, not too bad. It's the same color as your own hair, which is lucky. How about forgetting about your part for a while? Run down to the hall and see if Bumble's got the spots working yet. And bring me back a bottle of spirit gum for fixing Ross's beard."

They found Atlas parked outside a narrow building with

the words " Glencoe Hall 1886 " cut in the stonework over the door.

There were two more doors inside, one leading through to the hall and the other labeled " Kitchen."

" So far so good," Ross remarked. " We'll be able to have a cup of tea in the interval."

He pushed open the glass doors into the hall and groaned. " All things bright and beautiful! Dusty local dignitaries on the walls and a dirty old fireplace that's never used! These halls are always the same. They're always pompous and they always smell of mice."

Holly laughed. " Talking about smells, there's a terrible one floating round at the moment."

" It's the Major and his carbide," said Ross. " He's managed to get the curtains up. No stage lighting as usual. I'm always hoping against hope we shan't have to use those old spots."

Major Lumley put his head through a piece of dingy green curtain at the side of the stage. " Hello, you two. I've bought a packet of cream biscuits. Come and help me eat them. And just cast your eye over the star's dressing room."

Holly and Ross dived through the curtain. Behind it was another door into the kitchen. Ross looked around. " H'm," he said. " Let's pass on to the star's dressing room."

" This is it," said the Major.

" And the rest of the dressing rooms? " inquired Ross, grinning.

" In here," the Major grinned back.

" Well, it's nice and friendly all together around the teapot. We put on this act about dressing rooms, the Major and I, in every hall we go to. We've never had anything different yet. It's always the kitchen! "

The Major nodded. " I'm going out to get some more carbide for the spots. Biscuits are on the draining board."

They heard the hoarse rattle of Atlas gasping up the High Street.

" Let's look at the stage," suggested Ross. " And practice our moves."

" My moves for the *Rain Song* are easy," laughed Holly. " I just don't have any. We might go over that bit in *Sir Ralph's Revenge,* though, where you hurl me across the room when you can't get your own way."

She gazed out over the rows of wooden chairs.

" In less than eight hours they'll be full of faces. It's a ghastly thought. I've got my Sir Laurence Oliviers coming on again."

" Take a deep breath and tell yourself you're having fun," commented Ross. " Hullo! What's all this greenery sailing up the gangway? " He grinned. " Take a bow. An admirer is about to present you with first-night flowers."

" Compliments o' Parks and Gardens, sir," said a man in an apron. " Tae decorate th' stage. Whaur dae ye wish them? "

" What's the charge? " exclaimed Ross.

" Nae charge," replied the man. " 'Tis wi' th' compliments. A reciprocal gesture, as ye micht say. Ye bring us th' show, we lend ye th' ferrns. We allus dae it for foreign visiting bodies."

" Oh," said Ross. " Well, let's put them along the floor down there, shall we? " He jumped down off the stage. Holly was about to follow when she saw a face peeping at her through the side curtain.

" Are you the one who's going to sing? " breathed the face.

" Y-es, I think so," said Holly.

" I'll be glad to play the music for you. I'm Miss Millicent. Everyone calls me that. It'll make a nice change from teaching music." The faded blue eyes looked wistfully at

Holly. " I'm an exile, you know."

" Oh," Holly exclaimed. " That's terrible! Did you — if you don't mind my asking — did you escape at dead of night with nothing but what you stood up in, as exiles always do in books? "

" N-no. Not exactly," murmured Miss Millicent. " You see, I'm an exile from Surrey."

Holly paused. " I see," she said. " Well, I can understand how you feel because I'm an exile myself too for most of the year. You long for England where I am and I long for Scotland where you are. Isn't life just too awkward? "

" Yes, indeed," replied Miss Millicent, brightening a little. " But I do feel so far from civilization. Though they understand the importance of afternoon tea in Scotland, which is something. Well, now will you show me the piano? "

" I'm afraid there isn't one," said Holly. " I was going to sing — just into the air."

" No piano? " echoed Miss Millicent. " Dear me! That is very remiss of the authorities. I shall remark upon it at the first opportunity. But don't you worry, dear. I'll think of something."

She trotted off on the heels of the Parks and Gardens Department. Major Lumley put his head through the curtain.

" Come along, you two. It's nearly one o'clock. Lunch time. It's hot pot today, and we'll be in the hot pot if we're not there when it's dished up."

But when Holly received her plate from the Commander, she found she couldn't eat.

" I'm sorry," she muttered. " My mouth's dried up."

" Go on, eat it," Ross ordered. " You'll be all of a tremble if you don't."

" I'm all of a tremble now," retorted Holly.

" Don't worry the child," the Commander said calmly. " She can have an apple instead. I was frightened of my first audience once. And you can all give me your books. There's not going to be any last-minute studying. One thing only I ask of you, dear boys and girls. Pick up your cues quickly and take it fast. It's up to us to keep the audience awake. I shan't say another word."

They all meekly handed in their parts. The Commander took them into the Globe and sat on them. The Major crept into the shade under the caravan. " I shall sleep," he said.

" And I'm going down to the Loch," announced Pud, " to see if I can find some shells for the necklace."

Ross watched Holly fidgeting nervously to and fro.

" Get the cribbage board and the playing cards. I'd like a game. They're over the washbasin."

" Don't know how to play," said Holly, as she mooned past.

" Well, get 'em and I'll show you," replied Ross. Holly sauntered across to the Globe.

" Now concentrate on beating me," Ross went on. " You won't beat me, of course, but it'll take your mind off tonight to have a try."

Holly tossed her head. " I shall beat you easily."

The game was three all when Holly looked up to see Pud coming up the slope. " Any luck with the shells? " she called.

" No," groaned Pud, " and I walked miles and miles. But I met Andy. He was fishing in the Loch and he's lent me a boxful of stones with holes through them. They'll do fine."

" Tea squad forward! " boomed the Commander. " I

want to be at the hall by half past six."

Mrs. Menzies, the owner of the Claymore Hotel, was already seated at a table by the door when they arrived.

"Most good of you to consent to look after the tickets," beamed the Commander. "Your face at the entrance, my dear lady, will be an excellent advertisement for us."

Gentle Mrs. Menzies smiled. "I'm richt glad tae be of service," she said. "Th' hall looks braw wi' all th' greenery."

Holly glanced toward the row of ferns. "Hey! That wasn't there this morning," she cried, pointing to a black piano standing at the side of the stage.

The faded face of Miss Millicent peeped once more through the side curtain. "I hope it's all right," she called breathlessly. "I took the liberty of lending you mine. The Parks and Gardens dropped it by on their lorry."

The Commander bore down upon the shrinking figure. "I am without words, quite without words. Pud, prepare to carry out the commands of our new musical director."

Pud squeezed the timid hand of the new musical director.

"And give us something startling," went on the Commander, "not the same dull old gems from the same dreary old operas. Ross and Holly, get changed and ready for make-up." And she swept into the dressing room where Pud had already laid out the contents of the make-up box on a towel.

"Bumble, show Holly how to put her make-up base on. Open that cupboard door and dress behind it. That's the nearest we can get to respectability in this place."

She began pulling a skein of brown theatrical hair into tiny pieces. Ross had already seized the Number Five and had drawn large lines across the forehead and down his cheeks. He threw down the stick and began rubbing the grease paint into his face.

" D'you see, Holly," said the Commander, her quick fingers teasing the hair into fuzzy heaps. " Get it smooth in the cracks around your nose and mouth and well up into your hairline and taper it off down your neck."

Holly watched Ross's face change from tanned good looks to the fierce bronze of a buccaneer, a buccaneer with a square-cut beard touched up to match his auburn hair. She glanced at her watch. The hands were creeping relentlessly on toward eight o'clock. She felt her heart lurch at the sound of footsteps and voices in the hall as she stepped behind the cupboard door to wriggle into the pink, country-girl dress with its white muslin collar and cap.

" Five minutes! " called Pud, poking her head in. " Miss Millicent's going to start playing."

The Commander, the blue make-up pencil in her hand, remained transfixed. Holly's tense face relaxed into a grin.

" You did say you wanted something startling," she murmured.

The animated stomp of the " Cat Call Boogie " was throbbing through the noise and laughter.

" Miss Millicent disapproves," whispered Pud, " but she says it is her duty to be broad-minded."

Pud signaled the " Stand By " sharp at eight o'clock. Mrs. Menzies turned off the hall lights. Every seat had been taken. There were even several people standing at the back. Holly heard the rattle of the curtain rings and the sudden hush that fell upon the rows of chairs. She had found a tear in the side curtain and, to keep herself from panicking, had glued her eye to the peephole and was watching the faces of the people in the front row, ghostly faces without bodies they seemed in the reflection from the stage lights, faces lifted and eyes fixed upon the flamboyant figure of Ross bullying Holly's stage mother and father.

Now for it, she thought, turning away. Another half page of the script and they'll be down to, " I'll fetch her, sir," and then it'll be me.

Pud stood beside her in the darkness of the wings, the tin of dried peas for the rain effects ready in one hand, her copy of the words in the other.

" Don't let me down if I forget," implored Holly in a frantic whisper. Pud smiled. " I'm here all the time," she murmured.

" ' I'll fetch her, Sir Ralph,' " quavered the Commander, her face cowed and wizened, as she hobbled toward the wings. One last wild prayer, a last comforting squeeze from Pud, and Holly was on the stage and in the full glare of the lights.

She half saw the blur of faces below. She heard herself replying automatically to the harsh voice of Ross, as he seized her and flung her against the back curtains. A growl from the audience. Holly grazed her elbow on the floor as she fell and suddenly found herself wanting to growl too. She got slowly to her feet, turned to face Ross, and glared coldly into his eyes, now even more golden against the dark bronze grease paint. Her panic was gone. She was even able to remember calmly the Commander's last instruction to speak to the back row.

" ' Never, sir,' " replied Holly, lifting her chin and deliberately aiming her voice at the back row, " ' no man shall buy my heart.' "

By the time Sir Ralph had received the just reward of his evil deeds Holly was thoroughly enjoying herself. The curtain came down to a burst of appreciative applause at the sight of Sir Ralph's body sprawled lifeless across the stage. One man in a cap even got up and shook his fist at the corpse.

Holly's new-found confidence carried her jubilantly as far as her solo number. It was when she stood alone in the center of the stage to sing her songs that her fears returned. No one with her to help her along now. No being part of a team all pulling together. If she failed the Commander, the whole show would be ruined. Miss Millicent began the first bars of " Come to the Fair." Holly could see her beaming encouragement from behind the rows of ferns. The rustling died away. The blur of faces stilled.

And then Holly forgot everything as her voice sang its way to the roof and dropped into the intense stillness of the audience waiting to receive it. The Commander had allowed her to choose her last song. She gave them simply " Should Auld Acquaintance Be Forgot." As the gentle sadness of the words died away, the audience was strangely silent before a burst of clapping that nearly took the roof off the Glencoe Hall. Somehow Holly got off the stage, rushed through the kitchen, and, flinging herself into the Commander's outstretched arms, burst into a flood of tears.

" It's no good," she sobbed. " I've let you down. They didn't want to clap. They stayed quiet until they just had to clap out of politeness."

She gulped and raised her head and was amazed to find answering tears in the eyes of the Commander.

" Listen." She took Holly's hand. " They don't go on clapping out of politeness. Hark at them now. That silence is the greatest tribute any audience can give. Greater than all the noise that comes after. It's a sort of spell, and it takes time for them to awaken from it. Do you know, Holly, no audience has ever given me that silence. And you have received it tonight. Go back and take another bow."

Holly dried her eyes and went back. The Commander with her calm face unusually moved returned to her boiling kettle. Ross came up with Holly as she left the stage for the third time, silently pressed her hand, and kissed her.

She gave him a watery grin. " I'm awfully dry," she said. " The Commander's making the interval tea."

Pud had to ring the curtain up three times at the end of the program. The audience just kept on clapping. The Commander, flushed with the joys of success, sent Holly on again to sing them one last song.

"It's worth all the work when people thank you like that," Pud sighed. " It's the most wonderful sound in the world."

" And hearing that voice is worth all the dreary years I've spent driving music into reluctant little children," Miss Millicent sighed after her.

" And the only thing that's worth much to me at the moment," called Holly, as she helped Ross to roll up the silver bead curtain in its tissue paper, " is some really hot water to get this stuff off my face. I feel as if I've got one of those mud pack things on you see in beauty hints."

Ross, whose face had already returned to normal, grinned wickedly at Pud. " Shall we let her try hot water? "

" Wretch! " Pud cried. " Don't listen to him, Holly. Hot water'll make it worse. You want cold cream. Let me do it for you."

Altas bumped its way back over the old military road carrying a company well satisfied with the opening night of its summer season.

" Well, how d'you feel after your baptism of fire? " remarked the Major jovially as he handed around cocoa and biscuits.

" Simply wonderful," breathed Holly, gazing up through the clover-scented air to the vast dome of stars. " I just can't wait until tomorrow night."

Everybody laughed and nobody reminded her of the Sir Laurence Oliviers she had suffered such a short time before.

6

THE COLD WATERS OF INVERKENNETH

It was Sunday morning. The sound of Fort William's bells drifted away in a gentle clamor as Atlas, with the Globe rolling along behind, turned into the motor road running along the shores of Loch Linnhe on the start of the journey to Inverkenneth.

Ross, Holly, and Pud, jogging along together in the Globe, were flopped down among the faded red cushions, listening drowsily to the tinkle of the cooking utensils as they wagged together on the wall. Mrs. Menzies had given a theatrical party the night before in the lounge of the Claymore and they were all feeling droopy.

Pud was the first to come to her senses.

" Ross, wake yourself up. We've got that newspaper report to do about the show."

" Out into the storm with you," murmured Ross, turning over and preparing to fall asleep again.

Pud glanced with comical despair at Holly, who cast a thoughtful look at the slumbering Sir Ralph and tiptoed over to the water pail. She lowered the tea towel into the water and, climbing onto the table, sent the cold water cascading suddenly down his neck.

" Yow! " yelled Ross. " Who did that? "

The soaking tea towel still hung guiltily from Holly's hand. He made a grab. She ducked hastily under the table. Ross bent down to drag her out, caught his foot in the handle of the pail, and sent it flying.

"That's done it," Pud groaned, trying vainly to keep out of the way of the combatants. "Quick! Open the door and let it run into the road. There's Uncle Henry sounding the horn. Three times. We're wanted."

They all flew to the front window and looked down at the rear window of the car.

"What's going on?" mouthed the Commander, pointing toward the rocking Globe. Pud, Holly, and Ross with one accord raised their eyebrows, shrugged their shoulders, and exhibited every other sign of innocence they could think of.

"Perhaps that'll teach you not to snooze in the daytime," remarked Holly from the safety of the opposite side of the table.

"Shut up, you two, just for a minute," begged Pud. "e've got to get that report written for the local paper. I want to post it as we go through the next town."

Ross ran his hand through his wet hair.

"Hand it over, Pudding. I'll bring my great mind to bear on it if you'll make me a cup of strong black coffee." He began reading Pud's draft report.

"H'm," he murmured. "Not too bad. Reads quite well. . . . Wait, though. This bit won't do. You can't put that. . . . 'The piano was kindly lent and played by Miss Millicent Morton (or Warton).' What's the name in parentheses for? Surely she knows what her name is!"

"That's the point!" Pud cried. "She doesn't! I asked her surname. And she blushed and looked so flustered I wished I hadn't mentioned it. Especially when she said there was a mystery attached to her parentage. But when she did finally tell me, it turned out that on her birth certificate her name is given as Millicent Morton and her father's as Thomas Warton. Obviously just a mistake on the part of whoever made it out in the first place, but apparently it's practically ruined her life."

Holly grinned. " Poor Miss Millicent. She was so anxious about everything."

" Just put the two names in a hat and draw one out," suggested Ross, handing back the report. " And as I'm in a helpful mood, I don't mind assisting you with your case-book. It's about time you got started on the Ross Mordley mystery. Otherwise I'll have to take my custom elsewhere," he added, with a superior nod toward Holly.

She looked around for something to throw, but caught Pud's eye and drew her exercise book from under the cushions.

" Put down first what you know for certain," Ross said.

Holly wrote a description of the snuffbox: " Right in the middle is an ' E.' We're not sure if it's an ' E,' " she ended.

" Now you have to put down your deductions," Ross went on.

" It sounds like a theorem in geometry," Holly grinned, but wrote " Deductions " and underlined it.

" I know the Old Villain was a Highlander," she began writing. Ross looked over her shoulder. " You don't know that," he said. " You're only assuming it."

Holly kicked him under the table.

" You're a havering bletherskite," she exclaimed, " which being translated means a noisy windbag. I'm not going to assume it. I just know I'm right."

" Lopsided logic," Ross grinned.

" . . . because," Holly went on. " Now I shall make a list."

"1 His great-great-grandson Ross Mordley has the true Celtic coloring and fisseek."

Ross shouted with laughter. " Now, what's the matter? " Holly demanded. " Just let it pass," Ross choked. " Get on to item 2."

" 2. The Celts occupied the Highlands. 3. The owner of the box spoke the Gaelic, which was the language of the Highlands."

" Well, that's the lot," Ross said.

" No, it isn't," Holly frowned thoughtfully. " I want to add a bit about the ' Alone, Though Surrounded ' watchword. How's this? "

" Niall the shepherd thinks the watchword might mean ' surrounded by enemies,' or it might mean an island, as an island is alone though surrounded too. Niall says the man who owned the snuffbox was a proud and independent swankie. I am sure Niall has the second sight and really knows."

Ross raised his head. " What's the idea of calling my noble ancestor a swankie? " he demanded, grabbing a cushion.

" It's all right," Holly soothed. " It only means a brave, bold fellow. That's the lot. No more clues."

" You know," Ross said thoughtfully, " it really might be an island, especially as he was a pirate type. Very handy place to live."

The Globe rattled to a stop. Holly flew to the window and saw the Commander unwinding herself from Atlas.

" Halfway," she called. " We're stopping here for a large pot of tea."

" I'm going to sit in the open," Ross said.

Holly stretched out beside him on the grass. " Let's forget the island, if it is one, for a moment," she suggested, " and try to get back to the Old Villain himself. We'll track him down through you. What was your father's name? "

" Roderick Ross Mordley, born February 10, 1900, died August 29, 1950," said Ross promptly.

" Now your grandfather." Ross shook his head. " Sorry. No can do. Don't know a thing."

" Not even his name? " cried Holly. " Do try to remember something! "

Ross shook his head again. Pud drew the last drop of lemonade from her glass.

" Isn't the father's name given on the birth certificate? " she remarked. " It was on Miss Millicent's, wasn't it? "

Holly stared at her. " Of course. If we look up Roderick Ross, we'll find the grandfather's name and so on back to the Old Villain himself! "

Major Lumley had sauntered up with a jug of water for the radiator. " Not so simple, I'm afraid," he said. " You have to know the year the person was born or thereabouts."

" That's all right! " Holly said. " We know Ross's father was born in 1900."

" It's easy that far," the Major replied. " You can find the name of the grandfather but it won't say when he was born. You've got to know that to be able to look up his birth certificate to find the name of the great-grandfather and so on."

" I see," said Holly, considerably damped. " That's awkward."

" Pity Somerset House, where they keep all the records, is over five hundred miles away," replied the Major.

They had turned east and were rolling along the smooth motor road. Loch Kenneth lay silver and dark under the glooming heights on the farther shore. Holly was watching the cloud shadows on their rocky flanks when she suddenly let out a yell.

"Aunt Lottie!"

"Where?" said Pud and Ross, springing up.

"South Kensington," gasped Holly. "Quick! Who's got some writing paper?"

Pud felt in her pocket. "One scratchy bit left from my newspaper report and one rather grubby envelope. No stamp."

"Dear Aunt Lottie," Holly scribbled. *"I'm hot on the trail of a mystery. It's urgent. Will you visit Somerset House for me? I think it's in the Strand."* She sucked the pencil. "Give me your father's dates again, Ross."

She scribbled them into the letter and went on writing. *"I'm sending my ten shillings to cover your expenses. I think a trip to Somerset House would do you good, like a holiday. Love, dear, from Holly. P.S. After reading* The Hooded Horror Strikes Again *I've decided he's only an amateur. Not worth eightpence. Post your answer to —"* She paused. "Where shall I say?"

Ross considered. "Inverkenneth Post Office or forward to Fort Augustus."

They were nearing the gloomy fastnesses of Inverkenneth. A wall of mist hung over the precipices. Cowering at their feet lay the little town with its big metalworks. And, washing against it, the cold black waters of Loch Kenneth.

"What an eerie place!" exclaimed Holly, peering out. "And it's raining. I'm sure something horrid's going to happen here."

Atlas stopped under a clump of pines and the Globe slid to a standstill behind.

" What ever made us come to this awful town? " cried Holly.

" The awfulness of the town," replied the Commander. " People have to live and work here."

Holly flushed. " Sorry," she said in a small voice. " We've come to cheer them up, is that it? "

" That is it. We'll have to find somewhere to park out of the rain," went on the Commander. " It's going to stop the show if it doesn't soon hold up. We're doing it in the open here."

" And we don't know a soul either," the Major remarked gloomily.

" And I'll have a snoop round for some water," said Pud, picking up the pail. " I may find someone who'll take pity on us poor orphans."

She grinned and went off, a piece of newspaper over her head to protect herself from the rain which was now coming down heavily.

Holly felt a strange weight falling over her spirits. It all seemed so far from friendly Fort William and even farther from clover-scented Fluran. Not even a bird rustled in the dripping pine trees. Not a flower on the soaking ground. Holly felt tears pricking her eyes. She had a sudden overwhelming urge to fly to the road and run away, away to the light and the hills that were guardians, not frowning jailers.

And then, holding the tent pole steady for Ross, she looked at his unruffled face bent to the task of erecting the canvas. I should hate him to know how I feel. How I want to run away just because it's raining and ugly. Glancing up at the sad trees, she suddenly sang out, " ' It ain't gonna rain no more, no more.' "

They all took it up and suddenly Inverkenneth didn't seem quite so bad.

The fried eggs smelled friendly, and the ever-cheerful Pud was staggering up the road with the filled pail and a currant cake.

" A person with masses of children gave it to me," she explained. " And masses of wet washing on the line. She's invited us all to tea."

The Woman in the Shoe, as Pud called her, turned out to be the wife of a baker, a fat jolly woman.

" They're actors," Mrs. MacPhee proudly informed the six children who were staring with all their twelve eyes at the stately Commander.

" If it's still raining tomorrow, we shan't be," smiled the Major sadly. " We were going to present our program in the open. We've got nowhere fixed for an inside show."

" Dinna ye fash yersel'," beamed Mrs. MacPhee. " My Hamish is a braw one for haein' aroond when things look bad. Himsel's coming up th' path this verry minute."

Mrs. MacPhee was right. Hamish MacPhee, as thin as his wife was fat, his hair and face gray with flour, opened the door and stood transfixed at the sight of his wife's kitchen crammed with strangers. The children came to life and flew like a flock of birds to settle on their father.

" Ye'll not need tae be mindin' th' weather," he reassured them when all had been explained. " Leave me ma collar, wee lassie," he added, catching up the fat baby girl. " It allus rains here. We need tae stay on account of th' work. We'd be flittin' the morn's morn if we could. You've nae need tae fret. I'll fix ye up in th' recreation room at th' hostel."

" Will — will anyone come, do you think, Mr. MacPhee? " said Holly. " I mean, when it's so wet? "

" Come? " he echoed. " There's naught happens here but work. They'll be fichtin' for th' seats. I dinna doot but ye'll hae tae draw lots for th' tickets."

He was right. The news flew round Inverkenneth. There was no need for the Major to write any posters. The whole town demanded tickets. The Commander, good showman that she was, couldn't bear to disappoint her customers.

" We can positively stay only four nights," she said. " It means doing two shows every evening, that's all. We'll use the kitchen as a dressing room."

Holly and Ross glanced at each other and grinned.

" One thing only I beg of you, dear boys and girls," she added, " pick — "

" Pick up your cues quickly," they all chorused, " and take it fast! "

They picked up their cues quickly and they took it fast. They plowed through two shows a night, they packed the recreation room. Holly sang without music, the audience sang with her, and still it kept on raining. It rained solidly until the afternoon of their last day in Inverkenneth.

Holly was sitting sucking throat pastilles and looking out of the Globe windows on Thursday afternoon, when a thin watery gleam of sunshine struck through the smoke-laden air to the steaming ground.

" It can't be true. I thought it had gone forever. Oh, for some fresh air," she groaned.

" We'll walk back tonight after the show and try to get some of this smoke from the works out of our lungs," Ross replied.

" Five minutes," called Pud. " Hall's full. Crammed right up to the stage, if you can call it a stage."

Holly stood in her usual place behind the curtain. The buzz of conversation sank to silence. The Commander and Major Lumley began the cottage scene of *Sir Ralph's Revenge*. In strode Ross, his amber eyes flashing in his dark face, his riding whip cracking ominously.

And then something Holly had never heard before sprang from the audience. A choking gasp, a half-strangled shout, and the hasty scrape of boots on the floor.

She threw a lightning glance at the stage. By not more than the merest momentary pause did Ross show he had heard. He kept smoothly on with his part. Holly searched frantically in the folds of the curtain to find a crack wide enough through which to see the audience. Someone was stumbling down the center gangway, head bowed, making blindly for the door at the back. Holly could just see it was a man.

" What's up? " whispered Pud.

" I don't know," Holly breathed. " Some man taken ill or doesn't like the show, I guess."

" Look out! " Pud hissed. " Here's your cue coming up."

They discussed the mysterious disturbance during the interval.

" What could anyone not like in *Sir Ralph's Revenge?* " demanded Holly. " That man got up and went out directly Ross came onto the stage."

But by the time the second run of the show was over she had almost forgotten the incident.

Ross, wiping cold cream off his face, opened the window over the sink and peered out.

" It's still fine, if you can call damp ground and a murky mist fine. The trouble with this country is that when it starts raining it never knows when to stop."

" You're a Highlander now, remember," Holly laughed. " You'll have to wrap yourself up in a nice big plaid and pretend you like rain. Thank goodness Fluran isn't wet. Some of the islands have gorgeous weather."

She paused and began wiping off her make-up.

" Ross, if ' alone, though surrounded ' really does mean an island, how are we ever going to find out for certain? "

" Search me. Of course we could go and knock on all the front doors and ask if the Old Villain's in," Ross murmured.

Holly smiled sweetly at him. " A brilliant idea! There are only millions and millions of them. The whole of the Outer and Inner Hebrides besides masses of bits on their own."

She sat down suddenly. " Ross, it's absolutely hopeless. It's like looking for one special drop of water in the whole of the Atlantic."

" We've still got to prove it is an island," Ross observed. " If it is, I'll find it if I have to comb the whole lot one by one. I've got my teeth in and I'm not letting go."

Holly glanced at him from the corner of her eye. " How about getting Mother to design you a coat of arms? What do you think of a natty border of toothbrushes rampant with the words ' Up the Clan Molars ' picked out in silver? "

Ross whirled around and was about to administer chastisement, when a sound from outside froze them both into stillness.

" What ever was that? " he muttered, his eyes on the square of damp mist over the sink.

" Sounded as if someone hit against the window frame. A man, judging by the juicy curse. What a nerve! Sneaking around listening to other people's private conversations! Hop out of the side door, Ross, and have a look."

Ross darted along the passage and looked out. Holly flew after him. "See anything? " she whispered.

" Only a shadow vanishing in this dratted mist," Ross muttered. " I've a good mind to offer him a ten-round contest."

" Come on," Holly replied. " Let's finish changing and go for our walk, otherwise it'll be pouring again."

Ross nodded and poked his head out into the hall where the Commander was basking in the admiration of the canteen manager and directing the demolition of the temporary stage.

" We're going back by Lock Kenneth, Pud. You coming? "

" Can't," Pud called. " The Commander's going to help me wash my hair. I've put it off too long as it is. See you later."

The air was dank and still as they picked their way past the houses toward the road climbing the south bank of the Loch.

" It's not really much fun after all, is it? " Holly said in a low voice. " How creepy the water looks. It seems to be heaving but it doesn't make a sound. I don't like it when everything's so quiet."

They left the houses behind. The road climbed steadily through the thrusting outcrops of rock and the stunted bushes, which seemed alive and evil as they passed upward through the clinging mist. Holly kept glancing behind her. The curtain of vapor closed behind them and she could see nothing.

" I'm sure I can hear footsteps behind," she whispered.

Ross looked down at her, smiled, and, taking her arm, squeezed it comfortingly against him.

" It's the echo of our own feet coming back from the hills, that's all," he said. " Look, here's a big ledge hanging over the water. Let's stand on it and see if I'm not right."

They crept around the side of a rock buttress onto the ledge. " Now listen, " Ross breathed.

No sound broke the deadening mist. Below them the

oily water lay heaving smoothly in dark surges.

" I wonder how deep it is," said Ross, stretching out on the ledge, his feet hooked around the buttress. " Quite a drop too."

" Do be careful," warned Holly. " It's awfully cold and slimy here."

She glanced behind her to get a firmer grip on the rocky pillar, turned back and froze. Ross's body was sliding slowly and helplessly over the ledge. She remained paralyzed, her eyes fixed to his hands as they tried frantically to clutch at anything that would save him.

He gave a last cry as he fell. " Don't — come, Holly."

His voice dropped and was strangled in the plunge to the blackness below.

Numbly, Holly remained in the same position, staring down at the empty water.

" Dear Ross," she said aloud. " Don't — leave me."

The sound of her voice brought her to her senses. She tore her hands from their grip on the buttress, slithered to the edge, and, aiming for the dark spot where he had disappeared, went down after him.

She hit the water, sank, and rose to the surface again gasping. " Ross," she shrieked.

A strong arm caught her. " I told you not to come." Ross's voice was hoarse and shaking. " Can you swim? Kick your shoes off. Make for that flat bit."

Holly felt hot tears of relief running down her face as, half pushing her, Ross encouraged her to swim. Their clothes were heavy with water and threatened to drag them to the bottom. He pulled her at last onto the muddy ooze and they lay gasping and shivering.

" Come on, old girl," Ross urged. " You mustn't wait any longer. We must try to get back."

◈

The Commander, without a word wasted on questions, stripped Holly's clothes off and wrapped her in blankets. Pud raced to make hot tea.

"How's — Ross? " she gasped.

"He's all right," murmured the Commander. "Don't worry. He's terribly tough."

Ross came into the Globe, his dressing gown wrapped around him, and sat down beside her on the bunk.

"You all right? " he said, rubbing away at his wet hair.

"M'mmm," replied Holly. "Are you? You look awfully white."

"I always look that way after a bath," he grinned.

Holly managed a shaky smile. "Oh, Ross, why didn't you be more careful? I was afraid you'd slip. It was so horribly slimy."

"I didn't slip," Ross said. "I was pushed."

Holly started up, her pale face tense.

"Pushed? " she breathed. "How do you mean? There — there wasn't anyone but us on the ledge."

"I was pushed," Ross repeated. "Do you remember how I was lying? With my feet hooked around that buttress of rock. I felt something — or somebody — pressing hard against them. I slid forward. I couldn't help myself."

Holly shuddered. "We shall have to go to the police."

"No good," Ross said. "No one would believe us. Hanging over a slippery ledge on a wet misty evening? Near a lonely road? They'd tell us it was all imagination. Or carelessness."

He paused thoughtfully.

"Someone would have to loathe someone else very badly to do a thing like that. Or be very frightened of them."

7

THE WHITE PLAID OF SCOTLAND

THANKS to the Commander's speedy first-aid work, both Ross and Holly escaped the worst effects of their plunge into Loch Kenneth, though she insisted on Holly's sleeping in the Globe and staying there until they were ready to leave for Fort Augustus the next day. Ross, flapping about in a pair of the Major's trousers while his own were drying, peered through the windows and inspected her whenever she wasn't looking. Pud hovered around offering sweets and cups of tea.

Holly fretted and fumed at the forced inactivity and at having to lie down with all her clothes on in the middle of the morning. She flipped over the pages of her casebook.

" It's nearly a week since I wrote to Aunt Lottie," she remarked for the fifth time to Pud, who sat beside her with a halo of curlers in her hair.

" Shall I visit the post office again for you? " Pud said, putting down Henry the Eighth's tunic which she was darning. " I'll pop in and say good-by to Mrs. MacPhee while I'm out. We'll be leaving after dinner."

" Thanks, Pud, I wish you would," Holly sighed. " Give me that tunic. I'll try to finish the mending. Though I'm not very good at it, I'm afraid."

" Will you lend me your hood? " Pud went on. " I don't want to take my curlers out yet."

Ross flapped in to take Pud's place by the bunk.

" You look like something out of an early Charlie Chaplin film," Holly said.

Ross grinned, hitched the Major's trousers up a bit, and sat down.

" You can peel the potatoes," announced the Commander, putting her head in at the door and nodding at him.

Ross groaned. " I'm feeling very poorly. I need careful nursing, not hard work."

The Commander still had her eye fixed on him, so he picked up the potato bowl. Holly burst out laughing and the Commander withdrew.

Ross tested the edge of the peeler.

" Do you think it would be very difficult to learn the Gaelic? " Holly said suddenly. "It might come in useful."

" Not with a decent textbook and a dictionary. How about learning it together? Then we could pass rude remarks about people and they'd be none the wiser."

Holly smiled. " Let's have a try. Is that Pud's voice? "

Ross put the bowl down and looked out. " Yes, it is. And she's got someone with her. A craggy type with beetling brows and hands like hams. Where'd she pick him up? I'm surprised at Pud."

Holly tried to kneel up to catch a glimpse. Ross pushed her back and tapped her on the head with the potato peeler.

" Don't rush it," he remarked. " All in good time."

They heard the Major's voice and then footsteps approaching the Globe.

" An admirer," announced the Commander, coming up

the steps. " This is Mr. Murdo Dundas. He works at the factory and saw our show last night. Come in and meet our juvenile leads."

The man who had followed the Commander in was short and dark. He held out his hand after a searching glance at them both.

" I admired your show and wanted to meet you," he said without smiling.

After a second's hesitation Ross returned the handshake.

" I'm not an expert at anything but rock-climbing, I'm afraid," Dundas went on, " but I thought your stuff quite good. Who does your producing? "

" Mrs. Lumley, of course," smiled Holly. " Didn't you see the canteen manager introduce her at the end? "

Dundas drew in his breath. " Yes, naturally. It slipped my mind for the moment. You're leaving us soon, I suppose? "

" This afternoon," Holly said. " Are you a Scot? " she added. " You don't speak like one."

" A Lowland Scot, though my family has lived in the Highlands for nearly two hundred years. I'm proud of being a Lowland Scot," Dundas added in a level voice.

" Of course," Holly agreed quickly.

" There was no letter," Pud put in. " Perhaps it'll be at Fort Augustus."

" Fort Augustus? " repeated Dundas. " That's strange, isn't it? I was thinking of spending the week end in Fort Augustus myself." He paused.

" Come along with us," suggested the Commander.

" Yes, do! " cried Holly. " We'll tell him all about our casebook, shall we, Ross? "

A long, unsmiling look passed between Ross and Dundas. Then Ross nodded carelessly and turned away.

" What's the matter? " Holly asked, when Dundas had gone. Ross said nothing and continued to stare out of the window. " Don't you like him? " she added.

" No," Ross said. He picked up the saucepan and tipped the potatoes into it.

" But why not? He's quite nice."

" He is not," Ross snapped.

" I believe you're jealous," Holly laughed. Ross's face darkened. His eyes were so full of scorn that she drew back. " Jealous? " he said. " Jealous of what? "

Holly trembled. " Don't be so angry! Why do you hate him? He hasn't done anything."

" No, he hasn't done anything — anything that I know of. Tell him about our little mystery if you want to. It's yours as well as mine. Holly, do you remember when you sang for the first time at Fort William and I had that strange feeling — as if I wanted to remember something? I had it again when he came in. Only, Holly, don't — don't show him the snuffbox. I don't want him to touch the poor Old Villain's snuffbox."

Ross bit his lip. His golden eyes were dark as he stared imploringly at her. Holly saw with amazement the distress in his face.

" Ross," she said. " You can trust me. It's your snuffbox. Of course he shan't even see it. And I won't mention our casebook either if you don't want me to."

His breath relaxed. He got up. " I don't want to be unreasonable. You can tell him anything you want to. It'll make no difference in the end."

" What ever do you mean? " Holly said. " In the end? It sounds creepy."

" I don't know," Ross muttered. " There are some things you can't do anything about. Like storms and tornados.

You watch them coming and they catch you up and leave you alive or dead. But they have to come. You can't stop them."

Holly was silent. She thought of old Niall and the look on his face while he spoke about the watchword, almost as if he had been looking at the owner of it. She turned uneasily and looked out at the comforting figure of Pud re-pegging the trousers to the line. Ross speaks as if he had the second sight too, she thought. But what connection can there be between them? They've never even seen each other until a few minutes ago. I reckon it's just that their chemical make-ups don't mix or something. I loathe our math mistress and I couldn't possibly say why.

They discussed Murdo Dundas while they had their meal. He had introduced himself to Pud as she had come out of the MacPhees'.

" He's all right but I'm not struck," Pud said, her mouth full of jelly. " I thought it rude of him not to ask after Holly. He must have seen she was ill, lying there all wrapped up. He didn't even look surprised."

" And he didn't seem to remember the Commander's bow at the end of the show," Holly said.

" Perhaps he slipped out before the end," Pud observed. Holly and Ross exchanged a swift glance.

" And I'd already told him we were leaving for Fort Augustus. And directly he gets in here, he acts as if he didn't know. I reckon he just wanted a free ride."

The Commander held up her hand. " We mustn't be uncharitable, boys and girls. Mr. Dundas seemed quite pleasant to me."

And he continued to seem pleasant when he joined them just before two o'clock. He had brought Holly and Pud a box of chocolates and appeared to take such an interest in her casebook that, before she knew what she was doing, Holly had told him all about it.

She studied him while she spoke. Dundas had his eyes fixed on the floor and she could read nothing from his face.

"So you see," she finished, "the 'surrounded' bit might mean enemies or it might mean an island. I've promised to do what I can. Ross is a great friend of mine and I — wouldn't let any harm come to him," she added suddenly.

"Wouldn't you now?" said Dundas. He paused. "Were you expecting any?"

"N-no, not really," Holly smiled. "Those sorts of things don't happen nowadays. Feuds and so on, do they?"

She picked up Andy's stones which she was rethreading and joggled them idly in her hand.

"What are you doing with those?" Dundas exclaimed sharply.

"Making a spell!" Holly replied, laughing. "These are my witch's stones. See, I roll them about in my hands and make a powerful spell!"

Dundas stared at her, his eyes glittering. He recoiled and, turning abruptly, stared out of the window.

Holly and Pud exchanged a bewildered glance, but nobody moved or spoke again until they stopped for a cup of tea. Dundas seemed to have recovered his spirits. He and the Commander entered into an animated discussion as to the relative merits of crampons or nails for climbing boots.

Only Holly was pale and dejected, staring over to where Ross, who had traveled in Atlas, sat chatting with the Major. What is the matter with everything? she thought. Nothing seems the same since Mr. Dundas joined us. And then she shook herself crossly. Ross is making a lot out of nothing and so am I. What possible effect could a perfect stranger have on us, someone who'll go out of our lives forever when we get to Fort Augustus? Yet still that intangible cloud hung over the Globe. Her legs were shaky and she was glad to get back onto her bunk and be trundling on toward the time when he wouldn't be there any more.

Dundas invited them all to high tea at the Claymore when they were passing through Fort William. The sight of Ben Nevis, large and solid in the golden light of early evening, and the thought that she was near to *Sea Rider,* restored her flagging spirits a little. Ross refused the tea and went off to return Andy's stones.

They were crossing the road back to the Globe when Holly suddenly reeled and would have fallen if the Major had not caught her. Between them they got her into the caravan.

" Everything went black," she whispered. The Commander gazed searchingly at her white face and trembling hands.

" Delayed shock," she said. " I thought it would come sooner or later. You'll get back on that bunk and stay there until we reach Fort Augustus. Lying down too. Pud, make her some more hot sweet tea."

They had passed Laggan Locks with the Glengarry Forest a glooming purple against the sky when the Commander, who had been sitting beside Holly, suddenly straightened her back and smiled.

" Have you decided something? " Holly grinned weakly.

" I have. You're going back to Fluran for a week's rest. A change will put you right in no time. You've been working very hard."

" B-but the show? " Holly stammered.

" Perfectly simple. We've plenty of stuff we can do on our own. And there's that silly Aunt Dolly of yours, Pud. Doesn't she live in Nairn with too little to do and too much time to do it in? "

" I haven't seen her for years," Pud said.

" Nor have I, thank goodness," replied the Commander. " Go and look her up in my address book. I suppose I can endure her for a week."

" And — Ross? " Holly said.

" He's coming with you. Only for a week, mind! I can't cope with that fluffy female for more than a week. You can get an early bus back to Fort William in the morning. Do you think you'll be all right? "

" All right? " echoed Holly. " If Ross is with me, I'd be all right jammed in the pack ice at the North Pole! "

She saw Dundas watching her over the top of his newspaper but all she could think of was showing Fluran to Ross.

Pud, with the help of the scrubbing brush, was up at first light the next morning and down into Fort Augustus to examine the bus timetable. They were starting breakfast when she galloped back into the camp.

" There's one at ten to eight, getting to Fort William at half past nine. The next is at twenty to ten."

" We thought you'd gone fishing again," Ross grinned. " You're a very kind and well-cooked steam Pudding."

They just made the ten to eight. The Major bundled them out of the car and into the bus.

" See you Sunday. Don't forget to learn your new parts," Pud yelled, as the bus moved off.

Holly sank down to recover her breath. " I'll be glad

when we get to Fort William and I can put on my old tennis shoes. Pud's are hurting my feet. My only decent pair of shoes is at the bottom of Loch Kenneth."

There was a sudden movement a few seats ahead of them.

Murdo Dundas rose from his place. "Well now! Fancy meeting you two again. I thought I recognized your voices. I'm dropping off at Invergarry. Glad I met you because . . ."

The news that he was dropping off at Invergarry caused Ross to become almost civil.

"Yes?" he said.

". . . Because it really is an island Miss Holly is looking for. And I think I can help her to find it. I understand you're going on a sea trip."

"How do you know it's an island?" Holly breathed. Dundas smoothly ignored her question. "Do you know the coast of Jura?"

"No. Not really," Holly confessed. "I've mostly sailed around Mull and out north of the Firth of Lorne."

"It doesn't matter," Dundas replied. "I think you should try the northwest coast of Jura. Bear down past Oban, keeping to the coast, and turn under the south shore of Scarba. The — the island you want lies off the northwest of Jura."

"Thanks very much. But how do you know — ?" Holly began.

"You should have an exciting trip. There's a fine westerly blowing up. Here we are in Invergarry already!" Dundas broke in.

"Quick!" Holly begged. "What's its name? How do you know?"

But Dundas with a quick nod was on his way out of the bus.

" He really is the queerest type," Holly said. " First we think he's — well, an enemy, and then he's trying to help us."

Ross, now that Dundas had gone, allowed himself to smile.

They found *Sea Rider* carrying some water as a result of the rain. Ross whipped off the engine cover. Holly set to work bailing with an empty soup tin.

" That's that," she said at last. " How about some stores? There's plenty of nothing in the cabin."

" You go then," Ross said. " I'll give the boat a mop over and get it all shipshape by the time you get back."

" Good-oh," said Holly, leaping onto the landing stage. " Housework's not my strong point."

Sea Rider really had waked up by the time Holly staggered back with a loaded carrier bag. The engine ticked over sweetly. The portholes shone where Ross had polished them with the tea cloth, and the cabin reflected the sky in its clean wet paintwork.

" Brrr! " shivered Holly. " Drat Ben Nevis! It's always keeping the sun off. I'm glad I've got my dear, cozy old duffel coat with me."

" Deathshead Dundas was right," Ross commended. " There's a handsome westerly blowing up. But at least it'll be on our starboard side going down the Loch. What's the time? "

" Eleven o'clock," Holly said.

She saw the nine forty bus from Fort Augustus turning into the station, as Ross cast off and eased the boat from the steps.

" Hey! what's wrong with the ticket man? " Holly exclaimed. " He looks as if he's been stung."

The conductor was indeed acting in a most peculiar

manner. Dancing past his bus, he came galloping down the slope.

"*Sea Rider!* Are you two Sea Riders? Packet for you. From a Miss Pauline Somebody or Other. Tipped me handsome to try and catch you. Coming over!"

He threw the parcel across the lengthening expanse of water. Ross caught it. "Thanks," he called. "Much obliged. Carry on!"

The conductor remained standing and gazing after them, backed by the entire contents of the nine forty from Fort Augustus.

"Fine send-off!" Ross grinned, tossing the parcel over. "It's for you."

Holly glanced at the label. "At last!" she cried. "It's from Aunt Lottie. Isn't Pud a sport?"

She tore off the wrappings, which the wind immediately caught and blew away.

"Notepaper and envelopes," Holly said. "A letter and my ten shillings back. Let's see what she says."

"*My dear Holly, in view of the state of the notepaper and envelope which you addressed to me last week, I assume you are at the end of your resources.*"

Holly glanced at Ross. "Poor old Pud's last bit of paper, and weren't we glad of it!"

"Don't dither," Ross urged. "Read on and see if she's found out anything."

"*I appreciate your kind thought that perhaps Somerset House might be good for my health. I duly undertook the journey last Tuesday. In spite of the fact that the keepers of Somerset House regarded me with the gravest suspicions, I persevered in my inquiries on your behalf and found what you wanted.*"

"Good for you, Aunt Lottie!" Holly interjected.

" Go on," said Ross.

" The name of the father of Roderick Ross Mordley is Dugald Ross Regina Mordley. The birth of Roderick Ross was registered at Deal on 10th February, 1900. The occupation of Dugald Ross Regina is given as that of a lugger-man. The most suspicious of the keepers informed me that their records go back only as far as 1st July, 1837, and that if I wanted anything before that I should have to delve in the dust of some local church.

" I am returning your ten shillings, as I am not yet quite destitute. Many thanks for the thought. Your loving Aunt Charlotte Gordon."

Holly was silent for a moment. " Dugald Ross Regina Mordley," she said at last. " Your father was born at Deal in Kent and your grandfather was a lugger-man. What on earth is a lugger-man? It sounds like the worms people put on fishing lines."

Ross shouted with laughter. " They're lug worms! The lugger-men used to go out to the ships anchored in the Downs and act as messengers and so on in the days of sail. Their boats were called luggers. School of Navigation library! "

" So you're still seamen as far back as your grandfather. And still Scots too, with Dugald for a first name. And they didn't forget to tack the Ross on either. But what's this Regina bit? It's a sort of girl's name, isn't it? What a pity we haven't a clue when he was born, so we can look up your great-grandfather! "

" Don't worry," Ross said. " Something may turn up. What do you think about this tale of Dundas' that he knows it's an island we're looking for? "

Holly considered. " It wouldn't do any harm to see if there's anything in it. Our time's our own. I mean Daddy and Mother don't know we're coming, so they won't worry."

"I'm game," agreed Ross, "providing of course I have the strength left."

"All right, don't hint!" Holly laughed. "Take the tiller and I'll get us something to eat."

It was early afternoon when they hove in sight of Oban Bay.

"We'll hug the coast as he said. You haven't any charts knocking about, I suppose?"

Holly lifted the lid of the locker. "What's this? Map of the Western Highlands. Any good?"

Ross steadied himself against the cabin. *Sea Rider* was pitching in a freshening sea. He held up the tattered map.

"A museum is the place for this," he said. "It's torn right across the top of Jura. Still, it may give us a rough guide. This is where we are now."

He battled with the wind to get the map flat against the cabin roof.

"What did he say? Keep on through and then turn under the southern coast of Scarba? Wish we had an Admiralty chart to warn us of any pitfalls. This one's torn all across that part."

"I'm afraid I haven't a clue," Holly confessed. "Though Dundas didn't mention any pitfalls."

"I don't trust Mr. Deathshead Dundas," Ross replied grimly.

They had passed through Clachan Bridge. Ross steered toward the lee shore of Luing. Ahead across the narrow strait the gray and yellow precipices of Scarba towered to the clouds. He glanced uneasily at the sky. A lurid light hung below it.

"What's the tide doing?" Holly called from the cabin.

Ross glanced at the steely water. " Coming up to half flood, I'd say."

Now they were under the sheer dark cliffs of Scarba and running along through almost a dead calm. Ross beckoned to Holly.

" Hear anything? "

Holly cocked her head alertly. " A kind of growling roar. Like a waterfall. What is it? The sea howling in the Scarba caves? The wind in the corries? "

" It's too deep and continuous for the wind," Ross replied steadily.

" I — I don't like it much," Holly whispered.

" Go and make a cup of tea," he said.

Holly pressed his arm. " Oh, Ross, I am glad I'm with you. Though it sounds now like millions of stags roaring."

They were beginning the turn around the south end of Scarba.

" What did you say the top speed of *Sea Rider* was? " Ross asked quietly.

" Seven or eight knots if it's pushed," Holly said, watching his uneasy eyes. The wind suddenly hit them full in the face. Holly staggered against the cabin.

" I'd say we were running along at about thirteen or fourteen knots at this moment," Ross shouted through the uproar.

" Oh, no! " Holly cried, staring at the mast as it flew along against the heights of Scarba. " It isn't possible, Ross! You must be wrong! The engine just isn't capable of nearly that speed! "

" It would be — if the boat was being helped along," Ross answered.

Holly looked at him dumbly.

" By a fantastically powerful current," he added.

The words were blown back to her by the screaming wind. He nodded his head curtly at the cabin and Holly obeyed the nod. Her hands shook as she tried to light the primus. *Sea Rider* wasn't rocking any more. There was hardly any movement at all. It was only when she glanced from the porthole that her appalled eyes took in the speed they were doing. The cliffs of Scarba were flying past in a blur of spray.

" Holly! " Ross yelled suddenly. She dropped the kettle and flew out. She followed Ross's pointing hand and the blood drained from her heart.

Not two hundred yards on the left rose a tall foaming sea topped by curling waves. Leaping fifteen feet to the sky they fought together like demons, screaming and roaring. Racing pools of white scum fled from the boiling caldron.

" The — White Plaid — of Scotland! " whispered Holly. " We're in the Gulf of Corrievreckan! It's a trap! "

Sea Rider shuddered. It jerked madly as it caught a cross eddy. It writhed and tossed as inch by inch it was drawn nearer to the maddened pile of water. Lying over the tiller, Ross fought inch by inch to turn the boat away. Holly threw herself down beside him. Dimly she saw a glassy hole drawing the foam in a spiral down to the ocean bed, a gaping mouth, its throat open to suck in the shivering ship.

" I'll go over the side and try to hold the rudder. We're losing ground," she heard Ross shout.

" No! " she screamed back. " You'd never live in it. We'll both finish together if we've got to."

" Try — to remember — the Naval Prayer," Ross gasped.

Holly closed her eyes and bent the last of her strength on the tiller.

" 'O eternal God,' " she whispered against Ross's shoulder, " 'who alone spreadest out the heavens, and rulest the raging of the sea — be pleased to receive into — into thy almighty protection the persons — persons of us thy servants.' . . . Bless Daddy and — "

Ross felt her body fall limp against him. He slid her down into the well and felt the pressure easing on the tiller. The whirlpool, foaming horribly, had fallen away a little. To his straining eyes it seemed that the boat's head had turned a fraction inward toward Scarba. An eddy caught the boat and swung it in still more. In a moment they were racing along on the flying current out of the gulf as fast as they had, a few moments before, raced into it.

Ross's body was wet in spite of the cold wind. The cheated howl of the waters rolled after him but the tiller now answered easily to his hand. Whipping off the belt of his raincoat, he lashed it firm and catching Holly up carried her into the cabin. The kettle lay overturned on the floor. He grabbed it, dipped it into the pail, and turned the primus up as high as it would go.

He turned to Holly and, covering her up with the rug, began slapping her white face gently with his hand.

She shuddered, turned a little, and opened her eyes to find his anxious but smiling face bent over her. She flung her arms around his neck and burst into a flood of tears.

" That's b-better," gulped Ross. " Come on, dear old girl. Kettle's on the boil. How about some tea? "

8

LANGAN LIGHT

"It's a grand life if you don't weaken," roared Ross, in what he imagined was a fine baritone voice.

Holly gave a tremulous laugh, and pressed her hands closer around the comforting warmth of the teacup.

Ross stopped singing when he saw he had cheered her up.

"It was a trap all right," he said quietly. "That's the second time he's had a go at getting rid of me."

"Then you really think —?" Holly began.

"Yes, I do. It all fits in, now I look back at it. He was the man who —"

"Who shouted out and left at the beginning of the program," Holly put in.

Ross nodded. "And who hit his head on the window frame. We must ask after the bruise when next we see him."

"But why the feud, Ross? Why should he be so upset when he caught sight of you on the stage?"

"I don't know. But having seen me, he is so frightfully interested he actually has to come snooping around and eavesdropping. He hears something that confirms his suspicion, so he tries to tip me into Loch Kenneth. Well, we're going to play his game now. We're going to act all innocent and give him his head. Perhaps he'll get careless if he thinks he's dealing with a couple of lemons."

" If we see him again," Holly remarked.

" We will! " Ross observed grimly. " It's war from now on."

Holly looked doubtful. " Do you honestly think there's something in it? A feud between two people who've never met before, I mean. This isn't seventeen-something, you know." She paused. " Could it possibly have some connection with your Old Villain? I did tell Dundas about him and show him my casebook."

Ross shook his head. " He hadn't even met us when he came to see the show and tried to push me into Loch Kenneth. It wasn't until the next day you showed him the casebook."

" That's true," Holly admitted. " And so he tried to kill you just because he didn't like your face."

" He heard our conversation too, remember. What did we talk about? It might give us a clue."

" Mostly about the weather," Holly grinned. " And how, if ' alone, though surrounded ' meant an island, you were going to move heaven and earth to find it."

Ross stared at her. " Maybe that's the answer! Maybe it's a proof it does mean an island! And somehow he knows I have a connection with this island and doesn't want me to find it."

" And when he finds he can't drown you in Loch Kenneth, he comes out with his phony offer to help, knowing we'd seize on it because we haven't a clue where to look," Holly added eagerly.

Sea Rider was cruising along at dead slow. The wind still blew fresh over a heavy chopping sea. Holly's eager flush had faded. She sighed and put down her bread uneaten.

Ross looked at her anxiously. " Tell me what the White Plaid of Scotland is," he suggested. " It'll do you good to talk."

Holly smiled wanly. " You're a Celt. You ought to know the legend! Corrievreckan is supposed to be the witch's tub. She washes the Plaid of Scotland and tramps it clean there. The — the roaring is the water on the boil for the washing. And that dreadful white stretch of foam — that's the Plaid of Scotland. All clean. And white." She shuddered and buried her face in her hands. " I ought to have remembered where Corrievreckan is. I've only heard of it. I've never been here before."

" Once is enough," Ross remarked grimly.

Evening was setting in early. The sky hung gray, filled with low scudding clouds which tossed a fine mist of rain into the wind. Straight ahead lay a landless waste of water, heaving and tossing to the sky line. Behind them the frowning escarpments of Jura and to the starboard the long dusky line of Mull.

" Nice cozy view, I must say," Ross observed. " I can't see a welcome on the mat written up anywhere. And I certainly can't see this mythical island we've been chasing. Where do we go from here? "

Holly tottered out beside him and looked around the sky line. " Is it my imagination or is there a light away out ahead? It doesn't look like a ship."

" Wait a bit! " Ross exclaimed. " I believe it's a flashing light. It isn't dark enough to see for certain."

" The Langan Rocks are somewhere off Jura," Holly said. " The witch's cattle are supposed to walk about on the waves and she calls them home every night onto the

Langan Rocks. I think Daddy once told me Langan is the Gaelic for the bellowing of cattle."

"I'm getting the willies," Ross grinned. "I reckon Deathshead Dundas thought if we didn't finish up in Corrievreckan, we'd probably die of fright afterward. Are these bellowing rocks another menace we're up against?"

"There's a lighthouse built on them," Holly said. "Ross! That's what we can see. It's the Langan Light!"

"That's a comfort anyway," Ross replied. "At least we can keep out of the way of the stampeding cattle. Well, where do we go? Let's look at the map."

"That's Jura," said Holly, bending over it. "And there's Mull. You know, we're not all that far from Fluran. Let's try to make it tonight. I want to see them all."

Ross smiled. "So do I. I've had enough of boating for one day. Let's go."

He bent down to bring *Sea Rider*'s speed up from slow. The engine coughed, made a gallant effort, spluttered and died.

"Come on, old girl," Ross muttered. "Don't say you've fought and beaten Corrievreckan only to jib now."

This time the engine refused to try at all.

"Wet perhaps," Holly suggested.

Ross knelt down and went over it thoroughly.

"No juice," he said at last. "She's bone dry."

Holly flew to the fuel cans under the side bench and shook them one by one. A hollow rattle from all but the last, and from that only a light, sloshing gurgle.

They stared at each other. "A bare half can," said Holly.

"She must have gobbled it up coming through the witch's pot," Ross replied ruefully.

"I could have sworn I had them filled when we arrived at Fort William last week," Holly groaned.

"When you said they were full, I didn't trouble to look," Ross confessed. "It's beastly slack of me. I deserve to be court-martialed. We shan't get far on half a can."

They both stared over the water. The Langan Light flashed brighter as the sea darkened. *Sea Rider* bobbed about, ominously silent.

"The lighthouse," Ross said at last. "It's our only hope and I don't know if we'll even make that."

He poured in the precious half can of oil. The engine responded instantly.

"It'll be farther than we think. Distances are deceptive on water."

The tall shaft began to loom nearer. The beam lighted their faces as it swung around on its course. Now they could see tiny squares of light on the body of the shaft. Both of them listened anxiously to the chug of the engine. They were almost within hailing distance when with a hoarse gasp it choked and died once more.

"Not more than fifty yards to go," Ross groaned. "They'll never hear us from this far."

"The oars!" exclaimed Holly. "Unlash the oars from the roof of the cabin and we'll paddle one of them over the stern. It'll give us enough way to come a bit closer."

"Let me do it," Ross replied. "This light is here for a good reason — the Langan Rocks. Try to hang over the side and give me the clear if you can."

"Enough," Ross called. They were bobbing within twenty yards of the immense lower wall.

"Give them a hail," Holly urged.

Ross shouted at the top of his lungs. The wind caught his voice and tossed it away. They both bawled together. Again and again. Holly drew her duffel coat closer around her and sank down onto the bench.

" It's no good. The living room's almost at the top. See? That square of light under the lantern."

Ross threw back his head and stared up the wall. " We could try knocking on the front door," he suggested.

" Or whistling at them," Holly sighed.

Ross let out a yell. " The very thing! Don't say you've forgotten to bring it! "

" B-bring what? " Holly stammered.

" Your bosun's pipe. Where is it? Quick."

" In the front left-hand corner of my case," Holly said.

Ross dived to the cabin. " This'll carry through a howling gale."

He blew the " Attention " with all his force. The high rising scream of the whistle tore through the wind.

" Give it to them again," Holly urged, her eyes on the square of light. Ross blew the call again. They waited. Nothing happened. The beam continued to swing around in its steadfast circle. The sea still beat against the base, sending clouds of spray over the helpless boat.

" It's no good," Holly muttered, clinging to his arm.

" Don't give up yet," Ross said. " They've got to come down a lot of steps, you know."

Hardly had he spoken when a brilliant square of light cut into the darkness lower down the shaft.

Ross and Holly both screamed together at the tops of their voices.

" Anyone there? " yelled a voice.

They screamed again.

" I'm coming," roared the voice.

The figure of a man stepped out of the square of brightness and seemed to disappear into space. He reappeared, leaning over the base rail and waving a storm lantern.

" Who are ye and whaur are ye? " he shouted.

" Cabin cruiser *Sea Rider,* three tons. Just come through Corrievreckan. Requiring assistance," called Ross.

" Ye've whit? " The searching beam of the lantern found them at last and swept over their faces. Without waiting for a reply, the man ran into the ladder.

" Jax! Hughie! Come awa' doon," he bawled. " Ye canna approach any nearer," he called to Ross. " Say another five yards. What's th' length o' your moorin' rope? "

" Twenty feet all out," shouted Ross.

" Ye'll no hae enough slack wi' twenty feet. Coming over."

A shadowy coil of rope hit the cabin roof. " Make fast. Thon'll keep ye forty feet clear o' th' wall while ye're moored. Ye'll bang tae bits else agin our wall."

Ross leaped to the cabin roof. " All right," he called.

" We'll hae tae hoist ye in. I'll pull ye intae position."

Another rope appeared out of the sky and dangled against the silent engine.

" You first," Ross said.

Holly looked up to where the rope disappeared in the darkness.

" I'll try anything once," she grinned.

" Get a good grip. That's fine. O.K. Hoist away," Ross called.

Holly felt herself pulled clear of the boat. She swung perilously in the wind, cast a terrified glance at the empty space below, and the next instant was being lowered gently onto the landing platform.

" Blaw me doon if it isna a wee lassie," exclaimed the keeper, pushing his cap to the back of his head. Holly felt like throwing her arms around his neck.

" There's a wee lad down there still," she grinned.

" Och aye," he muttered, tearing his astonished eyes

away from her. " Lower th' hoist."

Two minutes later Ross stood beside them.

" Come awa' up. I'm Jamie Jordan. 'Tisna often we hae th' visitors tae oor wee hoose," he said, holding out his hand. " Jax was greetin' ower th' monotony not ten minutes since."

Holly took a deep breath and started up the vertical ladder toward the entrance room. The sea sank away. The wind blew stronger. And although she felt she was miles above the water, yet the great light circling above seemed no nearer.

Jax and Hughie met them and swung the heavy door shut against the wind.

" Whew! " Holly gasped. " That was an endurance test all right! "

" Ye've only juist started," laughed Jamie Jordan. " There's five more like that yet. Take it easy now, lass. Ye look gey fagged."

Hughie, the youngest keeper, was a fair shy fellow. Although he seemed unable to take his eyes off Holly, yet he hung back and it was Jax who leaped forward to help her up the stairs.

The living room was cozy and warm when at last they reached it. An oilstove winked redly. The table was set for supper. They lowered Holly into Jamie's comfortable old chair. Hughie ran to the alcove where the keepers had their kitchen and came back with plates of cold bacon and tomatoes and a teapot.

Holly relaxed thankfully. She looked around. Her eye encountered the soft thoughtful eye of a rabbit curled up behind the wire netting in an orange box.

" That's Hughie's," Jamie Jordon remarked. " And th' wee bird too." He lifted the cover of a cage standing on top of the orange box. " And th' wee hamsters," he added, pointing to another box on top of the cage.

Holly grinned at the pyramid of livestock.

" Dinna forget th' tortoises," Jax exclaimed. " When he came awa' back fra leave th' last time he hoisted in wi' a braw hen and twa tortoises."

" Where are they? " Holly laughed.

" Och, they pined for solid groond and Hughie had t' send 'em awa' back in th' mail boat."

Over supper Ross told them the whole story of their voyage, though Holly noticed he didn't mention Dundas.

The three keepers shook their heads in astonishment.

" I can scarce believe it," Jamie ruminated. " I wouldna attempt it except at slack watter wi' a followin' wind. An' tha says tha did it in th' teeth o' this westerly wi' th' tide at half flood an' in thon walnut shell? Ye musta had th' guid luck or th' guid seamanship."

" A bit of both, I think," Holly laughed. The food and warmth had revived her. " Do you know if there's an island off the northwest of Jura? "

Jamie shook his head. " A few wee rocky bits but naething of ony size. Why dae ye ask? "

Holly glanced questioningly at Ross, who nodded.

" We — we think we're looking for an island," she began. Between them they told the story of the casebook to the astonished keepers. " I wish I'd brought it up with me. I've got the snuffbox though."

She put her hand into her coat and turned the pocket up. And as she did so, the stone Robert had given her before they left for Fluran rolled out onto the floor. Hughie picked it up and laid it on the tablecloth. She handed the box to Jamie, who inspected it and handed it to the other keepers.

Jax shook his head. " Whit dae ye think, Hughie? Ye've got muckle facts tucked awa' in that dounce heid o' yours."

Hughie reddened. He looked at the box and laid it beside Robert's stone on the table.

" They're both on 'em seeds, miss," he said.

" S-seeds? " Holly stammered.

" This one," Hughie went on, becoming even redder at the sound of his own voice, " this one they call Our Lady's Kidney." He pointed to Robert's stone. " And this one wi' th' writing is Our Lady's Snuffbox. They're seeds of South American trees that get washed along from those parts by the Gulf Stream. I've heard tell they fetch up on one of the islands in the path of the Stream. And they don't get found nowhere else. Folks to split 'em open and fix a hinge as some chap's done to this 'un."

Hughie stopped, overcome by the length of his speech.

" Is it really true they can be found on only one island? " Holly asked. " Or just a tale? I mean, wouldn't the sea toss them about all over the place? "

Jamie shook his head. " Th' Gulf Stream's a wonderful thing. 'Tis a warm wide blue band o' watter flowin' through th' cauld Atlantic. When I was a mate on th' *Western Prince* we've been nosin' through a cauld winter wind an' in th' distance I've seen th' Gulf Stream lyin' warm and blue wi' a heat haze ower it. It doesna change its course or mix wi' th' watter on each side. It's true what Hughie speaks. Th' seeds flowin' wi' th' Stream would surely reach th' island he speaks of if it was lyin' in its path. Aye, th' Gulf Stream keeps its wee place in th' wide seas roond it."

" Then it really is an island we want! " Holly breathed. " And the island where they get washed up must be the island we're looking for. I see that now you've explained about the Gulf Stream running always in its own little channel. Do you know the name of the island? " she added.

Hughie shook his head. " I'm sorry, miss."

" Not even how to get there? "

Hughie's fair face became even more troubled.

" Where did Robert find the one that's called Our Lady's Kidney? " put in Ross.

" I don't think he said," Holly answered, trying to think. " He tossed it down to me and I believe he said something like: ' I've got you a present. It's a funny, long empty stone.' "

" Then Robert's our only link," Ross replied. " But he's a certain link if only he can remember."

Jax and Hughie being on night duty, Holly and Ross slept in their bunks in the tiny room below the light.

" It's like being a bird in a nest," she whispered to Ross.

" What sort of bird and what nest? " he muttered sleepily.

" A crow's nest, of course," Holly murmured.

Ross gave a strangled laugh which ended up as a yawn. " I'm too tired to think out an answer to that one," he said, turning over.

Holly smiled drowsily. Through the deep slit in the wall she could see the reflection of the great beam, a steadfast guardian of the waters beyond the Firth of Lorne.

9

LATIN FOR QUEEN

THE morning mists were melting in the early sunshine. Holly and Ross stood on the lantern balcony looking down over the coastline of Argyll and Kintyre, with Jura and Islay lying blue between.

" I'm sure we're swaying in the wind," Holly said, peering gingerly down the long sweep of the wall. " It's a ghastly feeling."

Ross laughed. " You'll feel more ghastly if you fall over. Look! There's Scarba and the witch's pot! "

" It seems harmless from here," Holly replied.

" Ye'd gae through her easy now," put in Jax, who was cleaning the lantern behind them. " 'Tis slack watter an' th' wind's doon."

" I can see some moving spots on Scarba. And on Jura. Red spots," Ross said.

" It's your liver," Holly grinned.

" Hae a see through this." Jamie Jordon came up the steps and put a telescope into Ross's hand. " Lookee! There's th' mist juist gaein' frae Fluran."

Holly gulped. " Let me look."

" The red spots aren't liver, they're stags," announced Ross, handing over the telescope.

" I can see our shack! They must be getting up already. Smoke's pouring out of the chimney! "

Ross glanced with a smile at Jamie Jordan. " I think it's time I asked for what we wanted last night. A drop of oil, if you happen to have such a thing in your store."

Jamie and Jax shouted with laughter. Even Hughie grinned.

" Langan Lighthouse is run on oil! I think we might hae a wee drap tae spare ye for thon walnut shell," Jamie gasped.

Ross bit his lip and joined in the laughter.

" Call again th' next time ye're passing through Corrievreckan! " Jax shouted, as Ross threw the Langan mooring rope up. " Guid luck, bairns."

Holly watched until Langan Light had dwindled and become once more part of the sea and sky.

" One day we'll go and return the oil they loaned us. We've been robbing the Northern Lighthouse Board," Ross grinned, as they headed out toward the Atlantic beyond Mull.

Holly was blowing the bosun's pipe full blast as Ross switched to slow and grounded *Sea Rider* beside another boat lying at the edge of the sandy beach.

" That's Jamie's father's boat. It's faster than ours. Daddy often borrows it in the summer. When I've pinched ours! " Holly grinned. " A Gordon! A Gordon! " she yelled. Leonie's fair head appeared at the door. Charles Gordon's followed. Robert shot out from under their feet and all three streamed over the grass. With a shriek of joy, Holly was gathered into their arms. She freed one hand from Robert's enthusiastic tackle and held it out to Ross.

" Come and join the family circle and be squashed to death too! "

Robert left Holly and fell on Ross. " Seen any ships? " he demanded. " I'm collecting ships."

" What about the train numbers? " Holly exclaimed.

" Oh — them," Robert said in a tone of contempt.

" Which way did you come? " her father asked.

" Had any breakfast? " added Leonie.

" Now, let's see," Holly said. " We took a short cut through Corrievreckan and had fried bread and baked beans with the keepers at the top of a lighthouse."

" Well, fancy that," her father replied. " And we had the prime minister of Mars to tea yesterday."

" Honestly, Daddy! " Holly protested. " If you don't believe me, I can prove it. How can I prove it? Because I'm not hungry and that proves I had breakfast in a lighthouse."

" A thoroughly feminine piece of logic," observed her father. " I suppose you can both manage a cup of coffee in spite of your alleged junketings with lighthouse keepers."

" I can jolly well see you don't believe us," Holly remarked when they were sitting around the table.

" Suppose you start at the beginning and then perhaps we shall get a more unbiased view of your exploits."

Ross and Holly between them explained once more all that had happened. But this time they left Murdo Dundas in.

" You see, Daddy, I didn't know whether to tell you about the Dundas part and Corrievreckan and the ducking in Loch Kenneth because I was afraid you'd clamp down on my casebook. But Ross said we mustn't hold anything back because you can tell lies by not saying things as well as by saying them."

Her father nodded. " If you'd left anything out for fear of what I'd say, I should have felt sorry. And just because you've had the courage to take the risk, you can both go ahead with your case. But no more Corrievreckans! "

" Daddy, you're an absolute saint. It's been hanging over me like a cloud. I feel just as if I'd been knocking my head against a wall and now I've stopped. And it's such a relief I could sing."

" Go along then! Let's hear this voice that's been knocking people sideways all over Scotland! "

" You don't think you've — well — imagined anything, darling, do you? " Leonie put in. " I don't mean the whirlpool. But this Dundas. It does sound rather extraordinary. He was a perfect stranger. You know what you are for jumping to conclusions! "

" That remark," Holly observed with dignity, " should have been addressed to Mr. R. Mordley. He picked Dundas out as an enemy before I'd even thought of it. And Mr. Mordley's signals instructor, who's a simply horrid man with a bark like an Alsatian dog, said Mr. Mordley was the most practical cadet he's ever had. So if you don't believe me, you go ahead and believe him," she added in a martyred tone.

Everybody burst out laughing.

" A most convincing speech for the defense," her father remarked. " From now on, we all officially believe in Mr. Murdo Dundas. Now be off and give *Sea Rider* a cleanup. I've got to catch the mail."

" Mail! Aunt Lottie! I've got a terribly urgent letter to write. Anyone got a bit of paper and an envelope? "

" You have! " Ross retorted. " Your aunt sent you some. I'll run down and get it."

" Daddy, I've got a terribly urgent thing to ask — " Holly began.

" Out! " said her father.

" Mother," Holly went on, preparing to attack Leonie. " What are you working on at the moment? "

" A set of water colors of Fluran's flowers," Leonie murmured, sorting out her tubes of paint. " I'd like to do a portrait of your Ross, but I never seem to get the time."

" You will when you've finished the Fluran book, won't you? You'll have masses of time to visit Edinburgh and worship all your beloved Raeburn portraits. Here's Ross back. Now, Mother, polish up your brains, there's an angel. Aunt Lottie says Ross's grandfather was Dugald Ross Regina Mordley. What do you make of the Regina bit? It's a girl's name! "

Leonie thought for a moment. " Creep into the house and ask Robert to lend you the new shilling Daddy gave him on Coronation Day. He's under the table being a very quiet ship's engineer."

Holly came back, undoing the dirty envelope where Robert kept the shilling.

" Now then," said Leonie. " The words around the Queen's head."

" Elizabeth Regina — " Holly began. " Latin for 'queen'! "

" Just so. Now if Ross's father was born in 1900, the grandfather would probably have been born in the reign of Queen Victoria. That's to say, somewhere after 1837."

" I can see that," broke in Holly, " but there was nothing special in being born then! I mean, to go and call the grandfather Regina just because a queen was on the throne! "

" Calm down and listen," Leonie said. " Why did Daddy give Robert that shilling on Coronation Day? "

" Because — because it was such an awfully special event and he wanted Robert to — to remember it, I suppose."

" Well? " Leonie said, smiling.

Holly stared blankly.

" Your mother means Dugald Ross was born on Queen Victoria's Coronation Day and they called him Regina because of it," Ross said.

" It's only a guess," Leonie put in hastily.

" Then I can find the date! " Holly burst out. " So Aunt Lottie can look up the great-grandfather! What day was Victoria crowned? "

Leonie and Ross shook their heads.

" Daddy! " shrieked Holly, bursting into the Black House. " Quick! Victoria's Coronation Day. Hurry! "

" June 20, 1837," replied her father. " And you can write it down a hundred times for interrupting me."

" Oh, Daddy! " wailed Holly.

" Out! " he replied.

Holly returned gloomily to her box of notepaper. " I've forgotten something. Aunt Lottie says their books go back only to July 1, 1837, and they told her she'll have to scratch around in church records for anything before that. We want June 20. What church records would Dugald Ross be in? "

" Deal probably," Leonie said.

Holly stared thoughtfully at Ross. " Dare I? " she murmured.

Ross grinned. " Have a go! She sounds a sport."

" Dear Aunt Lottie," Holly began, *" you are wonderful to have dug out Dugald Ross Regina. The trouble is I want the great-granddad now. I have a good idea our Dugald was born on 20th June, 1837, but it means scratching around in the dust. Do you think a nice trip to Deal would do you good? I don't know which church. Post what you find out if you find out to — "*

She paused. " Where shall I say? "

" Inverness," put in Ross.

" *To Inverness post office. Love, dear, from Holly. P.S. I am sending you my ten shillings for your expenses. Thanks ever so for the paper. I am using it. You are a sport.*"

She licked the envelope. " Come on, Ross. Let's go and take it to the mail and I'll show you to Niall. Maybe he'll teach us the Gaelic."

" That reminds me," Ross exclaimed. " I got you these in Fort William while you were enjoying your tea with Dundas. Found them in my raincoat pocket. Happy birthday! "

Holly took the Gaelic dictionary and the textbook.

" Oh, Ross, but my birthday's gone for this year."

" Then I'm sorry I'm late with the present."

Holly smiled and shook her head at him.

They found Niall sitting on his rock. He greeted Ross with a long look and a silent nod. Holly came straight to the point.

" Niall, we want to learn the Gaelic. Would you help us? "

The shepherd smiled ruefully. " 'Tis a dying language, lass. 'Tis gaein' frae th' Hielands like th' auld watchworrds. Th' auld order changeth."

Holly nodded. " I know, and I don't like the new order much either. Not when I'm in the Highlands anyway. I don't even like the telephone on Fluran really. It doesn't fit. Give us the Gaelic though, Niall."

" Ye'll hae tae woork gey hard. Th' grammar will fash thee sairly."

" Grammar? " echoed Holly, her face dropping. " Do we have to learn grammar? "

" Ye do," replied Niall sternly. " If ye'd hae th' Gaelic, ye maun hae th' grammar too."

They could see a yellow kite struggling halfheartedly in the air as they walked back over Cairnmor.

" That's Robert," Holly said. " He adores that kite but he can never get it very high. Daddy must be busy or he'd be hauling on the line for him. Come on. I want to catch Robert and ask him where he found that seed stone."

They galloped down the slope.

" Robert," Holly said, " would you like to be a detective like us? You can join if you want to."

Robert glanced suspiciously at them. " What do I have to give you if you let me? You can't have my shilling."

" We don't want anything. Only just tell us where you found this."

She held out the present he had given her at Fort William.

" The funny empty stone," Robert said. " I thought you'd throwed it away. You didn't like it much."

" I do like it," Holly replied. " Do try to remember where you found it."

" We went boating with Daddy and we landed on a lot of places, picking up bits of rock. Before you came from London."

" At which special place did you find it? " Holly urged.

" There was an island with another one joined onto it with sand; and the one joined on had a great high lump of hill and a great big stone arch where the sea came in to some white sand. I found the stone on the white sand."

" Do you know the name of the island, dear? " Holly asked.

Robert shook his head.

" Could you show it to us if we took you where Daddy went that day? "

" I guess so. This string's caught."

Ross took the kite, unwound the cord, and, shaking out the kite, he edged it high into the air.

Robert watched, enthralled. " You can get it much higher than I can. It's only a speck now."

He gazed up at Ross with his direct, gray eyes. " I'll show you the place. Only — I don't like the sea. I — don't mind being on it, but don't make me go in it. I don't like going in it."

" Robert, don't say that! " Holly protested. " Ross'll think you an awful baby."

Robert's face reddened.

Ross gazed up at the kite. " I couldn't bear it myself until I was ten. And I hated ice cream too. Now you can't keep me away from either. One day you'll put your toe in and find you like it."

" I'll show you the island any time you want," replied Robert, with a rare warmth in his normally suspicious eyes.

" Daddy! Daddy! Can we take a trip in the boat? Right away? " Holly cried, bursting into the house.

" Tomorrow," said Charles Gordon.

" T-tomorrow? ' 'wailed Holly, drawing up.

" Tomorrow," replied her father firmly. " Today you can clean *Sea Rider* and find some more fuel. And start on your Gaelic. And learn your part ready to dazzle Inverness next week."

10

CURSE STONES AND WHITE ROSES

LEONIE had made Robert a paper sailor's cap with " H.M.S. Sea Rider " written round it. He was sitting on the bench by the tiller, his eyes fixed on Holly, who was giving him last-minute instructions on " Correct Boating Procedure," as laid down in her *Sea Ranger Handbook.*

" Now, let's see," Holly was saying. " Crew, man the boat! Well, we've done that. I'm the Number One and you're the Sub and the Navigating Officer as well, because it all depends on you if we find the island. Ross is the Skipper. He's coming now. I do wish he wouldn't run. It's bad for discipline. Now stand up, Robert, and salute your skipper as he enters the boat."

Ross drew up sharply at the sight of his solemn-faced crew. He assumed the sternest expression he could muster and returned their salute.

" Cast off moorings." He jumped aboard. " Drat those tins of beans. That's the second time I've caught my toe on baked beans. Where's the quartermaster? I'll have him strung up the mainmast."

" You can't," Holly retorted. " We haven't got a quartermaster or a mainmast."

" Well, shove them into the cabin, old girl, so as I can

hit the deck, instead of my toe."

Holly was about to stow the offending carrier bag when Jamie, his hair flying and a pigeon basket in his hand, came pounding down the slope.

" Hey, Miss Holly. Will ye dae me a guid turn? Will ye tak' th' wee fowle wi' ye and loose her when ye get whaur ye're gaein'? She's a fatty. She doesna get th' exercise."

Holly leaned over the gunwale and took hold of the pigeon basket gingerly.

" Just open the lid and let her fly out, you mean? " she said. " Are you sure it'll be all right? "

Jamie nodded breathlessly. " Tak' hold o' her and push her intae th' air like. One o' th' laddies in th' mail boat tak's her tae th' mainland and gies her a fly but he's awa' hame tae Perth. Annie needs a fair long flight frae a different direction. I dinna get off frae Fluran frae year tae year mysel'."

Holly lifted the lid a fraction. Annie sat crouched among the straw with a suspicious eye cocked upward.

" She's not very keen, Jamie," Holly remarked. " She's turning her eyes up and thinking, ' What a hope.' "

" Tak' nae notice, Miss Holly," Jamie said cheerfully. " She haes a verra sad disposition. She'll dae fine. Dinna fash yersen. Juist toss her intae th' sky and she'll strike back tae Fluran."

" All right, Jamie. If you're sure she won't get lost. See you later."

The boy nodded and gave the boat a push off at Ross's signal. Robert put his eye to the pigeon basket and began an earnest conversation with Annie.

" Did your father say where they went the day they took Robert? " Ross asked.

Holly unfolded the worn map. " Yes. Round beyond Tiree and Coll as far as the Soise Group."

Fluran was dropping astern. *Sea Rider* turned in a wide circle as Ross swung it northward, its prow slicing pleasantly through the sparkling water.

" Now, Robert, look carefully," Holly said at length, as they approached the low green island of Tiree, with Coll a rocky hump at its back.

" Is this the one with all those sea birds screaming around it? It's got white sand. Steer around the north side, Ross."

" Not the one," announced Robert. " No hill."

" Coll's hilly. There it is. Is that the one? "

" No," Robert said. " No white sand."

Holly sighed. " All right, Ross. We'll have to go to the Soise lot. I hope Robert really knows and we're not on a wild-goose chase. Soise must be the best part of twenty-five or thirty miles from Fluran."

The warm, gold sun of early afternoon lay over *Sea Rider* as it plodded steadily toward the solitary ragged group.

" There seem to be quite a few islands here. How many do you make it, Ross? "

Ross stood on the bench. " The big middle one. One a bit smaller with the high, square hill. I think the rest are only bits and pieces of rock lying all around the other two. See if you can find them on the map. There they are. Just by your finger."

Holly frowned over the tiny print. " Forgotten islands, I'd call them. They're no bigger than dots on this map. The big one looks like Soise where the group gets its name from. The hilly one is Trill-something. Yes, Trillsean. The little ones all around the outside seem to be the Clach Mallach. The whole lot's grouped together."

" Look! people," Ross said. " See that straggling group of houses up at the end. Poor-looking lot. It seems a poverty-stricken place."

" Is this it, Robert? " Holly asked, as they swung in and along the south shore, with its long, raised beaches of blown shell sand. Robert looked doubtful. Holly saw him bite his lip, his face red and troubled.

" N-no, I don't think so," he muttered.

Holly let out an exasperated sigh. " Robert, you're a fraud. I don't believe you remember at all."

Tears welled into Robert's eyes. " I do remember," he sobbed. " I remember this place. We talked to a man with a lobster pot. But it isn't the one."

Ross glanced at Holly and her conscience smote her. " Cheer up, Navigating Officer, it's not your fault. We'll find it in the end if we have to comb the whole of the Western Highlands," Ross said.

Several women were scratching in a thin patch of ground at the southern tip. They looked up and stared. A group of men lounged against the side of a tumbledown house watching the boat without interest.

" Not a very bright lot," Ross remarked.

" They look thoroughly depressed and couldn't-care-less, don't they? " Holly replied, waving to the group and getting no answer.

" The north side's higher and rocky, too. It's got a waterfall! "

" I remember that," Robert exclaimed. " But it isn't where I found the stone."

" Why, the other one's a tidal island," Holly cried. " The tide's going out and there's a stretch of sand between."

They gazed eagerly ahead to the high, grassy hump of Trillsean.

" It's awfully steep, isn't it? The rocks go right into the

water. No landing place. It won't take us long to sail around this," Ross remarked.

They were approaching the farther seaward end of Trillsean, hidden by the tall, square hump.

" There! " Robert shouted. " There's the arch and the white sand. That's where Daddy landed. On that sand under the arch. I was right! I did know! "

" ' Alone, though surrounded,' " Holly whispered. " It really did mean an island. This island. Trillsean."

" H'm," Ross said at last. " So this is home sweet home. The only thing in its favor is that piece of water through the arch. It makes a fine natural harbor."

He threw his head back and gazed up at the ragged ends of the stone against the sky. " Tall enough and wide enough for a full-rigged barkentine to come in and anchor."

Holly stared at him. " I wonder — if the Old Villain had a ship. But he must have had! He was a smuggler and a pirate. Are you perfectly sure he was? Those sorts of people are only in books — "

"I know. In the children's library," Ross added. " Holly, you've got to believe me. It was the only thing Dad was ever certain about when he mentioned the Old Villain. Smuggling and so on was a — a historical fact. French gold and brandy and so on."

Robert, who had been watching them, was beginning to fidget.

" Let's do something," he said. " Let's eat. And I want to fish with my net."

" All right, dear," Holly said. " You've been very clever and we'll do what you want now. Let's go through the arch and eat our dinner on the sand."

" Not in there," Robert objected. " I don't like that

place much. It's witchy. Can't we go to the big one where the waterfall is?"

Holly hesitated. She looked longingly through the arch and then down at his face.

"All right. We'll go and eat on Soise."

Ross brought the boat to the edge of the sandy strait. Holly jumped overboard and splashed through the shallows. "Ross! The water's gorgeously warm. Not like the usual Scottish liquid ice. Why, of course! It would be. Hughie said it lay in the channel of the Gulf Stream. The one where the seeds were found, I mean. That's another proof it's the right island. I can hardly believe we've actually found it at last. Baked beans and bacon and tinned pineapple and evaporated milk to celebrate."

"Don't say it like that," Robert grumbled, as Ross lifted him over the water. "It makes my mouth go all juicy."

The offending carrier bag was soon empty. Holly swished the plates in the sea and announced that she had washed up. "How about letting Annie off now?" she suggested, remembering the pigeon.

Robert's lips drooped. "Must we?" he said. "She tells me things. We haven't finished what we were saying to each other yet."

They found Soise rocky and broken and covered with a layer of peat and coarse grass. A few thin sheep wandered over the humps.

"I don't know what Daddy found to be interested in here," Holly remarked. They were approaching the cluster of fields scattered near the shore. The women still worked at their raised patches.

"Aren't they queer?" Ross said. "Fields about the size of a dining room table."

"They're lazy beds," Holly replied. "Where the ground

is so poor that nothing will grow, they heap up the little bits of peat into pockets between the rocks and cover them with seaweed and so on to make them richer. Daddy says some of them are only big enough to grow a bucket of potatoes or a handful of oats."

"Poor wretches," Ross muttered. "Talk about scratching a living."

Holly stopped beside one of the women. "Hullo," she said pleasantly.

The woman straightened, her pinched face unsmiling. She brushed aside a wisp of hair, looked Holly up and down, and bent again to her work.

Holly reddened and moved away.

"I don't think much of the Old Villain's descendants," Ross admitted when they were out of earshot.

"I don't believe they belong to him. No pirate was ever miserable. The ones you meet in books are all rip-roaring types with beards. I do wish one of the people would speak to us. Let's try that man by the water. I'll ask him something and he'll have to answer."

"It's the lobster man we saw with Daddy," Robert whispered.

"Hullo," Holly said boldly. "What are you doing and what is that curved wall for out there in the sea?"

The man looked young, although his hair was bleached nearly white by the sun. He smiled at Holly and Robert.

"Thank you very much," Holly said.

"Whit for do ye thank me?" he replied.

"For looking pleased to see us and speaking to us."

The man grimaced and jerked his thumb toward the fields.

"They're a cauld lot. I'm aye glad when the lobster season's ower. I'm a bachelor and likely to stay one while I bide on Soise."

" You don't live here then? " Ross commented.

" Nae, God be thankit. I tend th' lobster pond. I'm aye glad tae get tae th' mainland. I dinna like th' Lowland Scots bidin' hereabouts."

" So they're Lowlanders. I thought they looked too short and dark for Highlanders," Holly remarked.

" Aye, an' Mad Mollie's th' lowest o' them a'. She owns th' place an' I rent th' lobster pond frae her. A queer one is Mad Mollie. Aye creeping aboot like a wee ghostie and feuding and fichting wi' her family. Most o' 'em's related to each other on Soise an' a' on em's got the blight like a potato. If I was afeered like this lot, I'd be reckonin' it was alang o' th' Clach Mallach. That's th' Gaelic for th' curse stanes yonder. Th' auld witches haed their wee stanes — "

" And they used to roll them about in their hands while they said their spells! " broke in Holly.

The man nodded. " Aye, that's th' hang o' it. I dinna ken how th' Clach Mallach got their name. But when folk hae sinfulness stainin' their hearts, their eyes see evil even in a wee piece o' th' Lord's innocent rock."

" Do you really believe in — curses and things like that? " Holly said, half laughing.

The man did not smile in return. " Th' auld curses were queer things. They live on frae generation tae generation in th' feafu' hearts o' th' guilty. They sour th' soul o' th' evil-doer until a savior arises tae wash awa' th' wickedness wi' retribution."

His face was stern as he gazed toward the tumbledown houses. " An auld evil lies ower this place. An auld debt lies unpaid. Aweel, tis naught tae me. I'm awa' up tae get ma piece and push off."

" Good-by then, Mr.— " Holly began.

" Just Hurdie, lass." He opened his basket. " 'Tis braw

tae see a happy face on Soise. Tak' this hame tae your mither."

Holly put out her hand for the fierce-looking lobster and managed to raise an appreciative smile.

Hurdie looked down at her, his fair face clear once more. " And here's summat for ye thysen. I dinna doot but ye're like a' th' other lassies that collect wee oddments and then leave them about th' hoose tae fash your mither! Ye're welcome tae this if ye'd care for it. I keep ma fishhooks in it. Aweel, nae doot th' fishhooks'll bide as weel in a matchbox. Maybe it doesna look much but 'tis summat o' a rarity."

He held out what seemed to be a replica of the snuffbox. " I picked it up once on th' sand of Trillsean. I've heard tell 'tis a seed o' some foreign tree. Ye canna find one anywhere else in th' whole of Scotland except on Trillsean. Would ye like it, lass? '

" More than anything else in the world," Holly said eagerly. " Because it proves something terribly important."

Hurdie twinkled at her and, shouldering his basket, set off.

" Ross," Holly said firmly, as they walked on toward the sand: " Hurdie finding that on Trillsean is the last cast-iron proof we need that we're on the right island. I wonder if there's anything in this curse and atonement business. Anyway, what he said about the Clach Mallach proves I'm right over Dundas' being superstitious. D'you remember what I told you? How Dundas nearly died of fright when I was joggling Andy's stones in my hands? "

" I'm not surprised over Dundas. He's got something on his mind. But these people. Why should they be scared? "

" Perhaps Hurdie was right and they've got something on their minds too. Guilty consciences."

Ross nodded thoughtfully. Robert, plodding along beside them, pulled at Holly's hand. " When can I fish? " he asked.

" Right now, dear," Holly said. " Look! There's a little loch. I expect it's where the waterfall comes from. And it's quite near the sand. Oh, the tide's in! The sand's covered between the islands! But it won't matter. Will you fish while Ross and I go and have a look at Trillsean? We'll pick you up in the boat."

Robert nodded and prepared to lower his net into the brackish water.

" We won't be long," Holly called. " Annie can stay with you for company. We'll let her off directly we get back."

They could still see Robert's distant figure as they turned in toward the hidden northern end. The sea lay now much farther up the ruined pillars and stretched in green calm within the natural harbor and even under the jutting rocks at the far end.

" What nasty luck! " Holly exclaimed. " The sand's gone. We can't go ashore after all! "

Ross switched to slow and they drifted under the arch.

" We can take the boat in under those rocks though," he said. " There plenty of head room if you lay the mast down."

" Why, it's huge," Holly exclaimed, her voice booming against the rock walls. " It's a real sea cave."

The light was by now only a dim roundness behind them. *Sea Rider* bumped gently.

" It feels like sand," Holly said. " Make fast to that jagged bit of rock. Then we'll see where it leads to."

" We said we wouldn't be long," Ross said doubtfully.

" And we shan't be," Holly urged. " It can't go much farther. Look at the distance we are from the entrance."

" All right then, I'm game."

They stepped out onto a rising slope of sand. The walls of the cavern had closed in a little to form a wide passage.

" I can hardly believe it's as big as this when you think of what it's like outside," Ross remarked.

" Lots of the islands are honeycombed with caves," Holly replied. " Think of Staffa and Fingal's Cave for only one. Gosh! Isn't it dark? I can't see a thing now. How much farther are we going to climb? "

" No farther, it seems," Ross replied. " We've come to the end. It's just a wall of stone."

Holly put out her hands and felt the cool surface.

" It's smooth," she said. " Feel. It can't have been weathered smooth right in here."

She drew in her breath sharply.

" Ross! It's moving! "

" I can't be," Ross muttered. " Where? "

" But it is! It's turning as I push it — like a revolving door. Feel. There's a space behind it now. Shall — shall we go in? "

" We might as well as we've come this far. Here, hold my hand. If we get separated, we've had it. I do wish I'd got my torch."

" We'll just have to feel our way," Holly murmured. " There can't be much more. The air's warm and dry. And terribly silent. I'd love to know how big it is. Perhaps the Old Villain was in here once. Shout, Ross. See what echo we get."

" Trillsean! " shouted Ross. " Trillsean! I've come back! "

His voice thundered, thinned, and thundered back with a falling echo.

"It's huge," Holly breathed. "Oh, Ross! What was that?"

"I didn't hear anything," Ross whispered.

"A kind of sobbing sigh. From farther off," faltered Holly. "Don't let go of me!"

"Bit of the echo that got left behind, I expect."

She could feel him smiling in the darkness.

"I heard that, though," he added sharply. "That clumping sound. I hope it wasn't the stone turning back into place. It sounded like it."

"Oh, surely not!" Holly shuddered. "Let's go back. We're not far in."

Their hands touched the wall.

"Was it here?" Holly whispered. "There's no hole."

"Farther along perhaps," Ross muttered. "It's awfully deceptive in total darkness."

They felt right along each way behind them. There was no hole now. Only cool dry rock.

Holly shivered. "Keep close to me, Ross. I think we're — we're shut in."

"Perhaps that shout of mine set it turning. It might have done if it's very finely adjusted."

"Robert!" she breathed suddenly. "What will poor Robert do? He'll be so frightened."

They began feeling their way along the rock, hand in hand. Their feet shuffled through dry sand and loose rock. Step by cautious step they edged their way forward.

"Ross," Holly whispered suddenly. "Can you — can you see a faint light? It's only the merest shadow of a glimmer."

They stumbled on.

"I believe you're right. The air's cooler," Ross muttered.

Holly shuffled to a halt. Far above in the cavern of inky blackness they could see a faint patch of light.

" I'm sure it's the sky," Holly whispered. " With a star."

" It's wonderful to feel the fresh air blowing down, anyway. A crack in the rock perhaps. It's all broken into boulders in this part. Here's a flattish piece. Let's sit down a minute. At least we can enjoy being a bit nearer to freedom."

He guided Holly to the stone. She sank down and leaned her elbows back. And immediately shot up again.

" Ross, there's another flat slab against my back. Farther up than the one we're sitting on. And — yes, feel — another farther up still."

She felt Ross turn sharply.

" They're steps, Holly, steps! "

He put his foot on the bottom slab and felt up as high as he could reach. " And they go on up! Let's try to climb them and see where they lead. At least we'll be doing something. I'll go first just in case. Be careful and hang on tight to the sides. It's very steep."

The steps continued to rise through the rocky shaft.

" It's like going up a ship's ladder," Holly gasped. " Only there's nothing to catch hold of."

Gradually the light became brighter. She could see Ross once more. And above him the sky, the lovely, free sky of early evening.

Ross's head went clear of the top. Holly heard him give a shout. He sprang out and hauled her up over the last step under some grass.

" Just look where we are! "

Holly blinked. " R-right at the top of Trillsean! On the square top of Trillsean! "

Ross flung himself down on the grass. " I don't care where we are, so long as we're free."

" And out of that inky blackness," Holly added, taking

great gulps of the sea wind. " It's just like a garden up here. Look at these wild rosebushes. They smell of sweet dry grass and summer! It's the little white rose of Scotland! "

Ross didn't answer. He was gazing at the sky, his hands behind his head.

" What's the matter? " Holly said, stretching out beside him.

" I was just thinking about that shaft," he murmured. " I wonder why it's clear. Surely it should be cluttered up with grass and earth and stuff. Even supposing the Old Villain made it as a sort of escape hatch, it's a good time ago. Hundred and sixty years perhaps. It would have got filled in with all sorts of rubbish during that time."

" You mean — somebody has been down there besides us," Holly said slowly.

" Maybe. And another thing. We came upon it from the bottom end. Probably if we'd been walking on top here, we'd never have found it. And even if we'd sprained our ankles in it, we'd have thought it was a pot hole."

" The somebody's not only found it but wants to keep it a secret. Because of all the grass over the top," Holly said. " But why? There's nothing down there."

" We can't be sure. We hadn't any light," Ross replied. And that stone at the entrance didn't come there by accident. It works on a pivot."

" Perhaps the Old Villain lived down there after all," Holly remarked. " He could have brought his ship in under the arch, all sheltered and hidden, and shut himself in behind that stone and been as safe as the Bank of England."

" With his crew as well, perhaps," Ross added. " One man couldn't handle a ship of the barkentine type."

" That cave would hold hundreds, judging by the echo."

" I'd like to know what happened to the poor old fellow," Ross said at last with a regretful sigh. " The tide's turned. We'd better fetch Robert."

" Ross, we can't! We haven't got *Sea Rider*. It's in the cave and no way of getting to it! "

" We'll go down to the lower rocks and I'll swim it," Ross said, getting up and taking off his jacket. " Ouch! My toe! "

Holly sprang up. " What ever's the matter? "

" Someone's pushed something into the ground and left a hole. I stuck my foot in it. Look. Here's another."

" What do you suppose they are? Nesting holes? "

" Don't know," Ross said, nursing his foot. " Shouldn't think so. They've been made by some instrument. The turf's been cut. And what's this powdery stuff around them? "

He picked up a handful and let it trickle through his fingers. " Looks like powdered rock."

" How far down do they go? " Holly said. " Put your arm in. It's longer than mine."

Ross lay full length on the grass. " It goes down the length of my arm, anyhow. And I can't feel the bottom."

" There are two more holes down here," Holly called.

Ross grinned. " Oh, well, let's climb down. The sooner we get the boat, the better."

11

HE MUST NOT BLOW THE LANTERN OUT

"YOU'LL find some biscuits and chocolate in the pocket of my jacket," Ross said.

He balanced himself on the rock, cut down to the water, and struck swiftly around toward the arch.

Robert, thought Holly suddenly. We've been ages. I wonder if he's scared.

" A Gordon! A Gordon! " she shouted at the top of her voice. " Robert! Are you there? We're coming."

She heard his voice answer faintly. He called something again but she could not hear.

He sounds as if he's crying, she thought.

And then she heard Ross call. Flying around, she saw him reaching for the rock.

" Where's *Sea Rider?* " she cried.

" Gone," Ross groaned.

" G-gone? How can it have gone? "

" The end of the mooring's there. I reckon the motion of the boat sawed it through on the sharp edges of that rock and it's been carried out by the tide."

Holly glanced swiftly around. " It's getting too dark to see. It might be anywhere. We shan't be able to go home. To think the dear old thing got us through Corrievreckan and now we have to go and lose it. I just can't imagine life without *Sea Rider*. And there's Robert. He won't understand about waiting until the tide goes down."

They ran across and looked over the water.

" Robert! " Holly cried.

A faint shout. " Holly — coming," she just heard him say.

They strained their eyes in the gathering dusk. Holly drew in her breath sharply.

" He seems to be in the water. He's walking in the water. But he can't be. He's terrified of it. Poor fellow."

Ross didn't answer. He ran down and was in the water again, streaking toward the distant figure.

Holly bit her lip as she watched the space lessen between his head and the Soise shore. She saw him stop and turn and then he was swimming slowly back toward Trillsean. And on his back rode Robert, the pigeon basket held clear of the water.

He'll never do it with that weight bearing down on him, she thought, her heart pounding heavily as she shared the ordeal with Ross. Very slowly he crept on. At last she was able to lean down and drag them both onto the rocks.

Ross lay gasping for breath. Holly fell on Robert, burst into tears, and hugged him.

" Mind Annie," Robert said. " She's hungry."

" He was on his way over to rescue you," Ross gasped. " I found him up to his waist in the water."

" You what? " Holly gulped.

" I heard you call. I — I thought you was frightened. And I tried to come," Robert explained. " And I'm hungry. And not afraid of the sea any more."

Holly regarded him with incredulous eyes. " I — you — " she began.

" Your sister is trying to say she thinks you are the cleverest, bravest boy she ever knew," explained Ross. " And she promotes you to Admiral of the Fleet on the spot."

Robert nodded. " I'm still hungry. And my pants are wet."

" We'll dry them on a rock. You'll have to run about in your nothings for a while. It's lovely and warm."

" I'm still hungry," repeated Robert.

" Where's your jacket, Ross? I'll give him some of those biscuits. We'll all have some."

" Not for me," Ross said, rubbing himself dry on his shirt. " That's all the food we've got. We shall be here until the tide goes down. Though I don't know what difference the tide going down will make."

" And no *Sea Rider*," Holly groaned. " I'd forgotten the boat for a minute. What's Daddy going to say? They'll be worried stiff when we don't come home. Can't we shout? "

" All the people live at the other end of Soise. And anyway I don't fancy they'd put themselves out for us. We could do with a telephone like Fluran's, even though it is new-fangled," Ross grinned.

Holly smiled sheepishly. " Yes, I know. The old order's fine when you know you can get at the new when you want it."

She crumbled a biscuit and dropped it into the basket. Annie eyed it suspiciously and then condescended to peck at it.

" There's the answer," Ross remarked, jerking his head at the bird. " Send her with a message."

Holly stared at him. " Do you really think she's a proper homing pigeon? She might get lost. Or refuse to leave us."

" We can try. We're no worse off if she won't go, are we? We'll want some paper. I've got a stub of pencil somewhere. And what'll we tie it on with? "

" We'll use a strip off the chocolate wrapper. I daren't

use it all because it would weigh her down too much. What shall we say? It's getting so dark and I'll have to write awfully small. How's this? 'Stranded on Trillsean, Soise group. Have lost *Sea Rider*. Tell Daddy. Love, Holly.' Doesn't it look terrible written down? I feel in my bones he's going to be very angry. And when Daddy gets angry he does the job pretty thoroughly."

Robert nodded dumbly.

"Now we've got to find something to tie it on with. Got anything in your pockets, Ross?"

Ross shook his head. "This jacket's almost new. I haven't had time yet to fill it with odds and ends."

Holly groaned.

"There's a little thread loose on one of my buttons," said Robert, craning his neck around. "Here on my collar."

"Not long enough to wind around and make a knot, old chap," Ross said.

"It's given me an idea, though," exclaimed Holly. She turned up the hem of her skirt. "I caught a bit of it on my heel and Mother made me sew it up. Luckily I'm not very good at sewing and it's all loose. Here's a lovely long thread."

Carefully she put her hands into the basket and lifted out the warm white body. Ross coiled the paper around the pigeon's leg and tied it on with the cotton.

"Now for it. Will she go?"

Holly held the pigeon on her hand, raised her arm in the air, and threw the bird as hard as she could in the direction of Fluran. "Home, home!" she cried.

Annie flapped heavily into the wind, turned and circled Trillsean once, and then rose steadily into the darkening sky.

"She's going southeast," Ross cried. "Good old Annie."

Robert burst into sudden, hot tears. "Why have you

thrown her away? " he sobbed. " She's warm and cozy. And good."

" She's going to Daddy and Mother with a message, dear. We'll see her again soon. And she's too fat anyway. It'll do her good," Holly said, with tears in her eyes as well.

A shadow swept with a sudden " kek, kek " through the sky.

" That's a peregrine falcon," Holly trembled. " They eat pigeons."

" Now then! " Ross said cheerfully. " Don't start worrying about her. She may be fat but I'll bet she's crafty. She'll get through all right."

He yawned. Robert saw him and yawned too.

" Let's find somewhere sheltered and have a nap. We can't do anything until morning. I'm terribly weary," Ross said, picking up his trousers. " There's a little hollow between those two rocks. It'll be warm. Come on."

He lay down and tucked Robert in beside him.

" I'll sit for a while and say some prayers for *Sea Rider*. I can't sleep. How long — would it take Daddy if — he came? "

" Allowing for the bird to get there? And if that boat he was borrowing is handy? Three or four hours perhaps, less if he goes all out and luck's with him. Though I shouldn't bank on it. Have a rest. We shan't get so hungry if we don't move about."

He put his jacket over Robert, who was already fast asleep.

Holly sat down on the grass and clasped her hands around her knees. Soise lay black against the dark apple-green sky in which a few stars were beginning to twinkle. The light, warm wind wafted the scent of the white roses over the grass.

Holly looked deep into the heart of the brightest star

and commended *Sea Rider* into the safekeeping of the God of sailors. Now I won't worry about the boat any more, she thought. It's no good asking if you're going to doubt all the time. I'll think of the Old Villain. He may have sat here on a summer evening, too, while his ship rocked in the archway. And he may even have fallen asleep in that cleft in the rocks where his great-great-grandson is asleep now.

Holly sat very still. Gradually a kind of dreaming peace stole over her, scented with white roses and the breath of the sea, as if the spirit of the first Ross were still guarding his island.

She got up and wandered to the base of the hill. Its summit lay a dark line across the stars. And then she noticed the light, a tiny wavering gleam, coming down the steep slope from the top.

Yet that sense of being cared for was still so strong upon her that she was able to look at it quite calmly. The light continued to swing closer. Holly stood still and waited. And then it was upon her and lifted up to fall full on her fair hair. And on to the withered face and sunken eyes of a shadow covered with a shawl. The shadow fell on its knees.

"Ye are his angel," came a whisper. "I've done nae wrong. He isna vexed wi' me. We are friends, he and me. I only gae tae stare at him. Sometimes I laugh. I wouldna harm one hair o' his bonny heid."

"Who are you?" Holly breathed.

"Naught but Mad Mollie," the shadow muttered. "I'm nae th' betrayer. I wouldna tak' aught frae him. Or sell him tae his enemies. Th' puir Lantern's gey lonely. He's chosen me tae be his dear acquaintance."

The creature bowed her head. "I'm tae be th' one that

pays th' debt. He will forgive all people, he says, when I be offered up."

The words, whispered with a kind of calm pride, made Holly shrink back in fear. Mad Mollie dragged herself closer.

"But 'tis th' black devil. He wants tae blaw th' Lantern oot. Th' curse willna be washed awa' if I let him. He mustna blaw th' Lantern oot. Mad Mollie'll be in th' dark without th' lightning's beams."

She held up her clawlike hand to Holly.

"Th' black devil came tae jeer. He forced me tae show him th' Lantern. He stole th' red stanes frae th' puir Lantern. I can but get this back. Th' black devil will come after me if he kens."

Holly felt a small hard thing laid into her hand. She stared down at the troubled heap in the shawl. What can I do? she thought quickly. Poor thing. She's talking gibberish.

"I'll take care of it for the Lantern," she said gently.

"He's stolen th' stanes frae th' Lantern and now he brings men tae stick their swords in th' Lantern. Nay, but I willna let them do it. Th' Lantern willna forgive if I canna pay ma debt. He'll come doon in his wrath and I shallna be his dear acquaintance."

She crawled close to Holly.

"Th' Lantern kens th' black devil's after blawin' him oot. He walked th' nicht. I heard him cry oot, 'Trillsean, Trillsean, I've come back.'"

Holly shrank away. "Are you — are you — a witch? How do you know he called out?" she breathed.

"I'm nae witch. I'm only Mad Mollie. I heard him cry oot. In th' dark. Wi' a huge cry. One o' his speerits was wi' him. I'm afeered. I'm afeered th' black devil will tak' him awa' frae me. Th' puir Lantern. He and me is dear acquaintances."

Clutching at her lamp, she burst into moaning tears and shambled off into the darkness.

Holly stood still, a creeping feeling in her back. She heard a splash. The sound brought her back to life. Turning swiftly, she saw the light gliding smoothly across the water toward Soise.

With a sob of fright, she ran to the cleft in the rock. The sound of Ross's quiet breathing reassured her. She lay down beside him and looked up at the bright star. Could I have dreamed it? she thought. Gradually once more the peace of Trillsean descended on her with the scent of the roses. The warmth from Ross comforted her trembling body. In a few minutes she too was asleep.

The wheeling stars swung onward through the sky. Below them the sea washed softly on the rock-bound shore.

12

SPARROW PASSING *SEA RIDER*

THE pale light of first dawn was creeping across the steely Atlantic when Holly awoke suddenly with the sound of a familiar call in her ears.

" A Gordon! A Gordon! " The cry echoed across Trill-sean's high ground and fell away to the sea.

For a moment Holly stared around. Whatever are we all doing here sleeping out without a tent and Robert with no pants on? And how dare strangers go about yelling the Gordons' war cry?

Remembrance flooded back at the feel of the red stone still clutched in her hand.

" Ross! Wake up! " She shook him. " Robert, wakee, wakee. I believe I can hear Daddy's voice."

Ross sprang up and was instantly awake and alert, his eyes searching the dusky sea around Trillsean. Robert rubbed his eyes and stared in astonishment at his naked-ness.

" Here! " Holly said quickly. " They're dry. Put them on."

" Are you sure you heard your dad or was it wishful thinking? " Ross grinned.

" I'm certain I did. I was just waking up. Perhaps it

woke me. There it is again! Coming from the other side! "

They raced to the southern shore.

" There he is! He's in *Sea Rider!* With Jamie's boat in tow. Shriek, everybody."

They shrieked and raced to the Soise end. Charles Gordon took his pipe from his mouth and waved.

" That's a good sign," Holly muttered. " He can't be too furious if he's smoking and waving. Look, the tide's been out and come in again. Oh, gosh! I'm faint with hunger."

" So am I," Ross admitted. " So am I," said Robert.

Charles Gordon had turned the boat's nose in and was seeking a landing place.

" Try here, sir," Ross called. " I'll wade in and act as a buffer. It's tricky with all these bits sticking out."

He rolled up his trousers and waded into the water. Holly pulled up the drooping hem of her skirt and followed.

" I reckon this channel's fordable even at high tide. We needn't have been so worried about Robert," Ross said hastily.

Holly caught her breath. " That would explain —

" Well, you two," called her father. " Come on board and be court-martialed."

" Wait for me," Robert shouted and flung himself into the water after them.

It took a lot to astonish Charles Gordon after twenty years of being a headmaster. But he was astonished now.

Holly couldn't help enjoying the expression of comical disbelief on his face in spite of the overhanging fear of his anger.

" He grew up last night," she stammered, hauling herself over the gunwale. " He's been wonderful. D-Daddy, before you — begin the lecture, where did you find *Sea Rider?*

Was — was it on its way home? "

" I found it caught between two of these rocky spurs on the seaward side. The paint's scratched but that's all. It would have been hidden from you on Trillsean, especially as its mast was down."

" Thank you, Daddy," Holly said meekly. " I'm ready for you to start now."

Ross clambered on board, lifted Robert in, and they sat silently dripping together on the bench, their eyes lowered to *Sea Rider*'s bottom boards.

Charles Gordon said nothing, but continued to smoke his pipe. Holly stole a glance at him from the corner of her eye. He was grinning with enjoyment over their downcast faces.

She sprang up, threw her arms around his neck, and burst into relieved tears.

" Daddy, you're a pure, undiluted angel," she sobbed, hugging him. " And I love you."

Her father put his arm around her and sat her on his knee, big as she was.

" I was young once," he murmured. " I climbed a church tower and couldn't get down. I got hungry too. There's a basket of sandwiches in the cabin."

Robert flew in after Holly but Ross still sat on the bench.

" I don't know what to say, sir," he began.

" Don't say anything, my boy," Charles Gordon said. " I trusted them with you and I knew they'd be safe."

Ross sprang up, wrung Charles Gordon's hand, and followed Robert into the cabin.

" Hurry up, slow coach," mumbled Holly, her mouth full of sandwich, " they're nearly all gone."

◈

Coll and Tiree lay behind them before they had finished telling the Trillsean story.

"Is it more exciting than your church tower jaunt?" Holly asked.

"Oh, much." Her father's face was grave. "You've had a mysterious cave, a phantom light, and a witch. I only had St. David's church in daylight. And a telling off from the caretaker."

"Daddy, you're teasing again. You make it sound like a book. There was nothing really mysterious about it, just an underground cavern like Staffa and a lamp like our storm lantern and an old person who talked nonsense."

Charles Gordon groaned. "Here am I all excited, trying to keep a bit of romance going in the world and all you do is strip all the glamour off and try to make it sound matter-of-fact and everyday!"

"Not exactly everyday," Holly admitted, "but there is a scientific reason for everything that happened to us."

She pursed her lips and tried to look wise. "And anyway, you get romantic caves and treasure and witches and things only in —"

"We know!" they all chorused. "In books from the children's library!"

Great billows of peat smoke were swelling out of the chimney stack as they climbed the slope.

Holly regarded the dense white column with awe and anticipation. "I do believe Mother's forsaken her paintbrush and is having a good bake-up."

She galloped ahead through the open door and enveloped Leonie in a bear's hug. Then she sat down meekly on her bunk.

"All right, Mother, let's get it over. You may start."

"But I have, darling," protested Leonie, her blue eyes

smiling through the clouds of flour Holly had scattered into the air. " Daddy and I haven't been to bed. We were a little worried, you know. When Jamie came galloping in sometime in the small hours with your message, I thought perhaps you'd be hungry when you got back, so I set to and made a cake and a steamed pudding for breakfast."

Holly stared dumbly at her. " Mother," she said at last, " I am at a loss for words."

" Well, that is a nice change anyhow," Leonie commented.

" What I mean," Holly said, " is — that besides being beautiful, you're an angel. May I lick the spoon? I've got a present for you somewhere."

She dived into the pocket of her duffel coat and held out the lobster.

Leonie looked with fascination from the lobster to Holly's coat. " Do you really mean you put a lobster in your coat pocket? Without any paper on it? "

" But, darling," Holly protested. " I had no paper! Only a toffee paper and that wasn't nearly big enough."

Leonie shook her head in despair. " Turn your pocket inside out and air it. Mind the flour! "

Holly stepped back too late. The dust and biscuit crumbs from her pocket shot into the mixing bowl along with the snuffbox.

" You blaze a trail of chaos and destruction like a plague of locusts! Here's your snuffbox."

Holly bit her lip and began dusting the flour off. She rubbed the lid and let out a yell.

" Ross! Oh, there you are. Look, it — it fell in the flour. I've wiped most of it off but the scratches on the lid are still full of it. We can see the design quite clearly now. It's a white rose! The white rose must be his emblem. Another proof he belonged to Trillsean! "

" I'm hungry," announced Robert. " And I can swim nearly. I'm going in the Olympic Games."

After breakfast, Holly gazed wistfully down at *Sea Rider* swinging at anchor. " I suppose we couldn't go for a — "

" No! " said Charles Gordon. " No more boating until Saturday when you return to knock Inverness flat with your theatrical achievement. You'd better go and pry some more of the Gaelic out of Niall."

" And judging by the amount of talking you've done at breakfast, you're going to get writer's cramp entering up your casebook," said Leonie.

" And we haven't learned our new parts yet," added Ross.

" All right," Holly sighed, " I give in. I know when I'm beaten."

In spite of " no boating," the rest of the week flew. Ross had undertaken the task of preparing Robert to be Scotland's champion in the Olympic Games. Robert became his shadow and trailed him in and out of the water until the moment when Leonie came down from the Black House to pronounce the sinister word " bedtime." Holly took one look at the grammar in the Gaelic textbook and shuddered. In the end it was Ross who determined to conquer it.

On Friday afternoon they were lying among the grass and flowers, hidden from the view of the prospective swimming champion, Ross deep in the textbook and Holly learning her part and trying to write up her casebook at the same time.

" Come out of your verbs for a minute," she begged. " I want to show you what I've put. Look, here's your family tree as far back as your grandfather. Perhaps when we get to Inverness there'll be a letter from Aunt Lottie and then we shall be able to add your great-grandfather here. That takes us as far as the Old Villain himself. Though I don't know where we shall get his name from. Perhaps it was just Ross. No! It couldn't have been because of that E in the snuffbox. We've got to search for a Ross E."

" We've found his island but we don't seem to have many more clues to anything, do we? " Ross lay back and stared at the towering clouds over Mull.

" N-no, I suppose not. Though I still feel we've missed something vital. Like the bit in a jigsaw puzzle that you always lose and the picture doesn't make sense without it."

" I feel just the same as you," Ross rejoined. " Though there's still the riddle of Murdo Dundas to solve."

" Oh, yes, I forgot him," Holly agreed. " Perhaps he'll turn up at our new show! Ross, do hear my part. I'm shaky in the last bit."

" Hand over the book then," Ross said, shutting the textbook.

Holly rolled onto her back and stared at the sky.

" D'you know, I can't really see you as Henry the Eighth? I think the Commander's done a bad bit of casting. I mean, you've got no tummy. Henry the Eighth stuck out ever so far in front."

" The first scene is Henry as a young fellow in his twenties. Look, it says here, ' Enter the king, slim and handsome.' That's me. Slim and handsome."

He darted from the path of the flying Gaelic textbook.

" The Major's taking the part in the later scenes with

the Commander as Catherine Parr, his last wife," he added, from a safe distance.

" But the Major doesn't stick out much either," Holly objected.

" Air cushion," Ross said, creeping back cautiously. " Pushed under his tunic and tied around his waist. It'll be your job to see to that. You'll be stage-managing the later scenes because Pud's the page boy."

" I'm longing to see dear old Pud again," Holly said. " I wonder how her Aunt Dolly's been doing and whether the Commander's gone mad yet. Let's go and say good-by to Niall before tea. We'll have to leave early tomorrow if we want to pick up the two fifty bus to Inverness."

The old shepherd greeted them with his usual grave smile and made them some brackish tea.

" So ye're awa'. Keep on wi' th' Gaelic, bairns. Find a few meenits for th' Gaelic and dinna forget th' wee I've learned ye. Lass, ye'll need tae watch th' grammar. Ye're weak on th' construction o' th' sentence. But th' lad's daein' brawly. I canna keep pace wi' th' lad. He'll be able tae read a bit o' th' Gaelic in no time."

" We'll be back soon," Holly said. " Perhaps we'll be able to bring our Scottish legends program over to Fluran to wind up the tour. You'd come and see it wouldn't you, Niall? "

" Aye," he replied. " I'd get a wee lad frae th' ferry tae keep th' sheep and I'd come tae see ma twa bairns play-actin '."

Holly got up and held out her hand.

" Ross, we'll have to go. It's past six. Don't forget us, will you, Niall? "

" Nay, I'll no forget ye."

He clasped Ross's hand and gave him a long look.

" Fare thee well and God speed thee, dear lad."

◈

The sun had not risen above the mainland mountains when they set out next morning. The wind blew fresh on the dark, glittering water. Faintly they could see the light of Langan still stabbing palely through the gathering dawn.

" Another fine day," Ross remarked.

" Yes, aren't we lucky? " Holly agreed. " Who dares to say it always rains in Scotland! Gosh, I'm frozen. I'm going to make a hot drink. And cook some more breakfast. We'll hang onto the cold lobster sandwiches for when we're in the Inverness bus."

" Talking of lobsters," called Ross, " there's a boat coming up on the starboard tack. I think it's our friend the lobster man returning from the mainland."

Holly flew out, a piece of bacon dangling from her hand. " It looks like him by his hair. Give him a hail and slacken speed a bit."

Ross cupped his hands. " Are you *Sparrow?* I am *Sea Rider*."

It was Hurdie. He lifted his arm in greeting as he passed, a delighted grin on his face.

" Thanks for the lobster. It's in our sandwiches," Holly shouted.

Hurdie waved. " 'Tis ma last trip tae Soise, God be thankit. I'm gaein' fishin' up Loch Kenneth for a few weeks. How ye daein '? "

" I met that Mad Mollie person you told us about on Trillsean," Holly shouted back.

" Did ye now? Tha wee ghostie hersel'? " Hurdie's hearty laugh rang across the widening space between the two boats. " She's a queer one is Mad Mollie Dundas."

Ross and Holly gulped. " Quick! Put it to slow, Ross." She darted to the roof of the cabin.

" What did you say her name was, Hurdie? " she yelled.

" Dundas," came the fading voice of Hurdie over the water.

They flopped to the bench and stared at each other.

" This puts new life into the casebook," Holly said at last. " Or could it be just a coincidence? "

" I doubt it. Coincidence can't be stretched too far. Deathshead said he was a Lowland Scot, remember, and Hurdie told us all the people on Soise were too."

" Yes," Holly agreed. " That just about clinches it. I'll get some breakfast and we'll think out what it means."

" The first thing that sticks out a mile," Ross began a few minutes later, a plate of bacon and fried bread balanced on his knees, " is that he must have recognized me for some reason, although he had never seen me before. And having recognized me and realized from eavesdropping on our conversation that we were looking for an island in which he was very interested as well, he takes steps to get rid of me. Which means I must be standing in the way of something he wants or is planning to do. Either that or just plain fear, as we've proved he's superstitious. But that leaves us with the question, Why be afraid of me? I don't think a type like Deathshead would kill on superstition alone."

" You mean that although he may be superstitious deep down inside him, he's mixed more in the world than the others have done on Soise," Holly put in.

Ross nodded. " And having got that veneer of civilization, I think he'd used his head as well as his instincts."

" You mean — ? " Holly began.

" I mean I don't think our Deathshead will be crude. It will be a delicate, refined piece of extermination, well thought out to cover his own tracks. Yes. I'd say superstition perhaps but with a good concrete reason for it. And now that we know Mad Mollie's a relation of his — "

"His mother, I'd say," put in Holly. "I saw her face pretty clearly in that lamplight and she had the same deep-set piercing eyes and that frowning forehead. Perhaps they're both cracked."

"They seem to have some sort of fear complex in common. And probably, if she's his mother, his home is Soise as well."

"That's it," Holly replied quickly. "And perhaps they're both afraid of the same thing?"

"Something to do with Soise or Trillsean, you mean. Do you remember what Hurdie said about some old curse and someone would have to do a bit of atoning before it could be wiped out? Perhaps they're both afraid of the curse. If there is such a thing hanging over them, of course. We don't know anything for certain."

Holly put down her plate and stared at him. "I seem to remember Mad Mollie saying something about that. She said she had been chosen by the Lantern to be offered up to wipe out the debt. And when the debt had been paid, the Lantern would forgive all people."

Ross frowned. "How frightfully creepy! Do you suppose this debt she talks about is her word for a curse. And is it an old or a modern curse?"

Holly stared at the sea. "Hard to tell," she replied. "Daddy told me some of these queer old types get time all out of perspective and they talk as if something that happened hundreds of years ago took place only the day before yesterday. And Mad Mollie was queer all right! I wish I could remember what else she said. I just thought it rubbish at the time. Let me think. It may be terribly important to us. I know she started off by muttering, 'You are his angel.' Do you think she meant guardian angel? And if so, whose? All the time she kept on about the Lantern as if the Lantern was a person. And how the black devil was after blowing the Lantern out. And how men had come to stick swords in the Lantern after the black devil had forced her to show him the cave and he'd found the stones. Ross! She was coming from the top of Trillsean and you thought the shaft had been used recently! Do you think she was down there when we were? She said she heard the Lantern call out and she used the very words you shouted to test the echo! It frightened me terribly at the time. I almost began to believe in witches. That'll show you how scared I was! "

Holly paused. Ross was listening intently, his hand guiding *Sea Rider* under the towering cliffs of Mull.

" Let's have another look at the stone she gave you," he said.

Holly dived into her pocket. " Isn't it a lovely glowing red? It's very like the stone in Mother's engagement ring and that belonged to Daddy's mother. The stone in that is a ruby."

" A ruby? " Ross remarked. " But that's a precious stone! Where does our Lantern get rubies from? "

" There must be something else she goes to visit in the cave. Now I remember! She said if the black devil blew the Lantern out, she'd be in the dark without the lightning's beams."

Ross shook his head. " Don't start telling me there's lightning in an underground cave! "

" And another thing," Holly cried. " This black devil she talked about. Do you remember Hurdie said they were all relations on Soise and Mad Mollie was always quarreling with them? It sounds as if she hated this black devil for what he was trying to do to the Lantern. Do you suppose — "

"The black devil is Murdo Dundas, her son?" put in Ross.

"Yes! And he's trying to force her to let him do something and she won't because of the Lantern. And he can't do it unless she gives him permission. Hurdie said she owns the island."

Ross's eyes lightened to their sparkling gold. "I reckon you're right, Holly."

"And he doesn't want you to find the island because it'll stop him getting what he wants. Though we don't know why it'll stop him, do we? That's why he sent us on that wild-goose chase and hoped we'd get drowned in the whirlpool. But what does he want?"

"To blow the Lantern out!" Ross grinned. "More coffee please. And no more talking. We've got to concentrate if we want to catch the two fifty Inverness bus."

The three-quarter chime was striking over Fort William when Ross brought *Sea Rider* panting up to the landing stage.

Holly nudged him. "Don't look now but do you see what I see propping up the wall of the station?'

Ross took a quick glance. "Mad Mollie's curly-headed boy!" he muttered. "Deathshead himself!"

"Just there by accident, I suppose," Holly grinned from behind the engine cover. "What are we going to say? Do try to be civil, Ross, we might learn something."

"Leave it to me," Ross murmured. "Watch me trot out Ye Olde Worlde Charm."

Dundas met them as they came up the steps. "Well, if it isn't my two young acting friends," he exclaimed with well-feigned astonishment.

"This is a pleasant surprise," Ross replied, with every indication of having found a long-lost friend. "Awfully good of you to meet us. How ever did you know when we we were arriving?"

Dundas gave him a fleeting glance.

"I just happened to be here," he said shortly. "Well, Miss Holly, did you find your island?"

"Oh, yes, thanks," Ross put in cheerfully, before Holly could open her mouth. "But we must have misheard your directions. We went a bit out of our way and had to take a short cut through Corrievreckan. Stupid, wasn't it? With a westerly blowing too! Still, we found it in the end. And all's well that ends well, isn't it — sir?"

Holly glanced anxiously at Ross. I hope he's not going to offer to polish his shoes, she thought. Ross's eyes were gazing up at Dundas with an expression of simple, child-like trust.

"Holly met such a nice old lady too on the island, who I'm sure would have sent you her love if she'd remembered it. I think she must have been your mother. You're so alike."

Holly drew in her breath. She saw a dark cloud pass over Dundas' eyes.

"Really?" he said. "And did the dear old lady see you, my friend?"

"No," Ross replied with a charming smile. "I was asleep."

Dundas' face relaxed. "You were mistaken. Unfortunately, I have no mother. She died when I was young."

Ross's face dropped in sympathetic concern. "Then she's been dead a very long time? I'm so sorry I mentioned it," he stammered sweetly. "Did you remember to blow the lantern out, Holly? We'll have to go. I'm afraid we're catching a bus. May we get in touch with you if we have any more problems? You've been too helpful so far. Good-by — sir."

He dragged Holly with him and stopped the Inverness bus, which was just turning out of the station.

Holly just managed to hold herself in until she reached her seat. Then she collapsed. Peal after peal of laughter rang through the bus. The sound was so infectious that everyone smiled, then chuckled, then burst out laughing too. The astonished conductor took a quick look at himself in the mirror between the windows to see if he was the cause of the mirth. He shook his head sadly over his rocking passengers.

Ross sat meekly grinning to himself. "I enjoyed that. I never thought dear old Deathshead would amuse me. He knows now."

"Knows what?" Holly said, wiping her eyes and getting out the lobster sandwiches.

"That we're on the right track. I gave him two unmistakable hints. The next move is his. He'll come into the open now perhaps."

Holly shivered. "At least we can be sure he isn't on this bus," she exclaimed. "We can eat our sandwiches in peace."

"I wonder why he was so anxious to know if the dear old lady had seen me. And so relieved when he heard she hadn't," Ross said thoughtfully.

13

A REVOLUTION IN FRANCE

PUD, with a bulging carrier bag of stores, met them at Inverness, a Pud browner and more freckled than ever.

"Feeling better?" she grinned at Holly. "You look fighting fit."

"Pud, it's wonderful to be back. And I've such masses to tell you. Still, we've got all the evening."

Pud shook her head. "We haven't. Rehearsal all evening. And it's going to take a good time to reach camp. We couldn't get the one we wanted by Loch Ness, so we're up in a field off the Culloden Road. Know your parts? We've got a lovely hall here."

"How did your Aunt Dolly get on?" Ross asked, as they crossed the suspension bridge over the River Ness.

Pud groaned. "She wanted to stay on to play the piano for Holly, but Aunt Caroline convinced her Holly sounds better without music! And that she'd lose Uncle Percy if she didn't hurry back. We've had an awful week in Fort Augustus. I'm hoarse from prompting her. She bounces onto the stage, shows her teeth in a tooth-paste smile, and thinks she's going to be whisked straight off to Hollywood on the strength of it. She's got lovely teeth but nothing else."

She leaned gloomily over the bridge and stared at the fast, clear water. Ross put his arm through hers.

"Never mind, Spotted Dick, you've got us back now, you lucky thing."

Holly frowned at Pud. "Push him over. The rail's not too high. He's getting ever so conceited."

Pud laughed. "The water's not deep enough to cover him. Isn't it running fast? And what a lovely golden color. Like the cairngorm stones in that shop just below the High Street."

"It's been running through peat, I expect," Holly said. "It looks lovely, but it's horrible for making tea. I'd like to see that shop, Pud. Cairngorms are my favorite stones."

"It's on our way," Pud replied, picking up the carrier bag. "Shall we have a cup of something while we're here? I'm weary."

"Let me take that nose bag," Ross remarked, thrusting his rucksack over his shoulder. "What ever's in it?"

"Tins," said Pud.

"N-not spaghetti, I hope," Holly muttered.

"No," Pud said gravely. "We got the spaghetti in yesterday all ready for your return. Here's the shop. We can pretend to inspect everything while we have a rest. The High Street doesn't stop climbing once it starts."

Holly gazed at the cut and polished quartz and agate and the winking yellow cairngorms. Ross moved over to look at the lumps of rock where the stones still lay embedded in their raw state.

"That's the one I'll have. When I've got five pounds, that is," Holly remarked, pointing down at the black velvet where a huge cairngorm lay like frozen amber water.

"Do you know," Pud whispered, glancing across at Ross, "I think they are just the color of his eyes."

" I thought that too," Holly said. She put her hands in her pockets and stared at the stones. " I suppose they know all about them in the shop. Ross! How about going inside and showing them Mad Mollie's ruby? Come in and back me up."

They were only just in time. The assistants were preparing to lock up. Holly put the stone on the counter. " I don't want to buy anything. At least, I do, but — Can you please tell me what this is? "

The young man glanced appreciatively at her and picked it up.

" We get a lot of people coming in here and thinking they've found a fortune in the hills," he smiled. " This is a poor form of ruby. Not a good specimen, I'm afraid, although it's been well cut and polished."

" Are they valuable? " Holly asked.

" In some cases, yes. Rubies can be very costly. If they are good ones. The best come from Burma. You won't find many fine ones in Scotland. This is Scottish ruby. I'm sorry I can't be more encouraging."

" Then they wouldn't be worth — worth digging for if there were a lot in a heap? "

" You wouldn't be likely to find a lot in a heap, I'm afraid, miss. And even if you did, they'd be worth very little if they were like this one."

" Are they found in the Cairngorm Mountains like those in the window? " Holly said, picking up the ruby and putting it into her pocket.

" Cairngorms are a form of quartz. Rubies and sapphires are crystallized aluminum oxide."

" Thank you," Holly replied, trailing slowly out of the shop.

" I'm sorry it wasn't valuable," Pud said sympathetically.

" I don't care about that," Holly replied. " I'm just trying to think where I've heard about aluminum oxide. Was it at Inverkenneth where the works are? "

" Fort William perhaps," Ross suggested. " That has a works too."

" Fort William! " Holly exclaimed, stopping suddenly. " That rings a bell. Something to do with *Sea Rider*. I've got it! Coming down Loch Linnhe! We passed a steamer and Daddy said it was on its way to Fort William from France or Spain with bauxite for making aluminum. He said bauxite's terribly precious and that it was aluminum oxide."

She stared at their blank faces and let out a yell.

" I've got it! I've got it! " she cried and burst into the first few bars of " Begone, Dull Care."

Ross and Pud dragged her from an enraptured Inverness High Street into the nearest teashop. They found a quiet corner and put a cup of tea in front of her.

" Now," Ross said, " what have you got? Besides hysterics? "

" Just you listen," Holly whispered. " I believe I know what Murdo Dundas is after on Trillsean. And it even makes sense of what Mad Mollie said! "

" Well, if it makes sense of that, you've certainly got something. Tell us quick," Ross urged, his elbows on the table.

" Do you remember she said that after the black devil stole the stones from the Lantern, men came and stuck their swords in and he wanted to blow the Lantern out? "

" Yes, go on," Ross said, intent eyes on her face.

" What I reckon happened is this. Deathshead must know a good bit about rock formation and geology and all that bilge, being an expert rock-climber. Agreed? "

Ross nodded.

" He would also know a good bit about making aluminum, being at the works. I reckon when Mad Mollie had to show him whatever is in the cave and he saw the cut rubies, he had a snoop around the rock face and found some more in their rough state. Knowing they were a form of aluminum oxide, he immediately suspected the presence of bauxite or at least the possibility of it. Bauxite's very precious, remember. He may even have recognized traces of it in the rock from which the cave has been cut."

" He'd be able to recognize it in its raw state because he's seen it at the works," put in Ross.

" That's it," Holly agreed. " So he gets men over with drills to make trial borings. Remember the holes you fell into? Mad Mollie said men came and stuck their swords in the Lantern."

They stared at each other.

" And she meant he wants to mine Trillsean and tear it to pieces when she said he would blow the Lantern out," Holly went on eagerly. " That's what they're fighting about. She owns it and he can't do a thing unless she gives the word. She doesn't give a hoot for the bauxite. All she's thinking about is the Lantern, whoever or whatever the Lantern is."

" Yes," Ross said thoughtfully. " It's quite a reasonable theory of yours."

Holly sprang up, knocking her teacup flying. " Ross Mordley, you're a stuffy, conceited, stuck-up, pompous old — lump. You sound just like Daddy when he gives me that See-Me-in-the-Head-master's-Study voice! It's not theory. It's fact. I'm just as right as I was when I said you were a Highlander and you said I was only assuming it! "

Ross grinned at her. "All right, old girl. It's fact. Just let me wring the worst of the liquid out of my trousers and we'll see where this leads us."

Pud dived under the table and began mopping up the pools from the teashop carpet with her handkerchief.

"We would choose a place with expensive furnishings," she groaned from underneath the tablecloth. "Next time we'll patronize a serve-yourself."

"Now then, where were we? We've decided it's very probably—I mean, quite definitely bauxite he's after. But why pick on me? I don't want the beastly stuff."

"I haven't thought that far," Holly admitted. "And her saying she'd be in the dark without the lightning's beams must mean something too. I still think the reason you're in it somewhere is because they're both superstitious. I don't know why. Just a feeling. Aren't we getting on? What price the poor old Hooded Horror now? He wants pensioning off."

Pud sighed. "I haven't understood a word you've been talking about."

"Sorry, Pud," Holly smiled. "We'll have a bang-up midnight feast in the tent tonight and I'll explain everything. Mind the tea! It wasn't me that time. Is that someone you know?"

Pud had jumped up and was waving frantically.

"It's Atlas going by! Uncle Henry thinks we've lost our way and has come to find us, I expect."

Ross unwound his elbows from the teacups and sprang across to the door. Inverness High Street was treated to another enjoyable diversion as Ross galloped down the middle of the road trying to catch up with the old car, which he didn't do until it had reached the other side of the river.

The Commander greeted them with a relieved sigh and the pleasant prospect of sausages and onions.

" Another week of Pud's silly Aunt Dolly and I should have been put straight into a Benevolent Home for Aged Actresses. Catherine of Aragon, you look a lot better. I hope you know your words."

" ' Indeed, your Majesty, I am come posthaste to do your bidding,' " replied Holly gaily, sweeping her a wide curtsy.

" You know some of them, I see," the Commander remarked, twinkling benignly. " Though we shall doubtless find some weak spots after supper. Bumble, put that carrier bag down. You look like a pile of Christmas shopping. There's a letter for you, Holly. In the big saucepan. I put it there so as I shouldn't forget it."

Holly snatched off the lid. " From Aunt Lottie, the angel," she cried, flying out to Ross, who was knocking in his tent pegs. " I do hope she's had some luck."

" Open it quick and see," Ross replied. " I'm getting quite interested in my dead and dusty relations."

Holly ripped open the envelope. Out fell her ten-shilling note once more.

" ' My dear Holly,' " she read to an eager audience, *" ' Thank you for your kind thought. Kensington has indeed been remarkably stuffy lately like most of its inhabitants, so I acted upon your suggestion and journeyed to Deal to sample the sea air. I am afraid I did not even catch a glimpse of the English Channel as I spent the entire day viewing the architecture of Deal's sacred edifices. . . .' "*

" What's an edifice? " Holly said.

" She means churches. Go on," Ross urged.

" ' I regret to inform you I have now a permanent squint caused by peering at countless parish registers, though

doubtless in a good cause. I could not, however, trace any entry in the name of Mordley. . . .'"

" Oh," groaned Ross and Pud.

"' . . . *But at St. Bonaventure's, which has a most delightful man in charge, elderly and I gather unattached, I found an entry that has the same Christian names and is perhaps the one you are wanting. It is, by the way, an entry of baptism, not birth. The baptism was that of Dugald Ross Regina Macaudré, aged 2 years 4 months, which took place at St. Bonaventure's on 20th June, 1837. There was a note at the side of the entry in faded ink which I was able to decipher with a magnifying glass kindly loaned by the delightful person. It reads: " This child was born in Rue des Emigré, Paris, on 3d February, 1835, the mother being Susanna Macaudré, nee Heathcote, and the father Revolution Ross Macaudré, French soldier, killed 1836 Strasbourg fighting for Louis Napoleon. The woman Susanna Heathcote was formerly nurse to the Montvernon family during their sojourn in France and has now returned to their employ on the loss of her husband."*

"' *I took tea with the helpful bachelor and returned to Kensington for a good rest. I return your ten shillings, as I took a cheap day return and so was able to afford the fare myself. Your loving Aunt Charlotte Gordon.'"*

Holly folded the letter slowly. She and Ross exchanged a long look.

" Revolution Ross Macaudré, French soldier," she said quietly. " Your great-grandfather, the Old Villain's son, a French soldier. How ever did he come to be in France and fighting for the French? And what an extraordinary name. It's worse than Regina. Ross, I wonder if Revolution commemorates anything too? The trouble is, we don't know how old he was or even if he was born in France, though the Macaudré bit, where I suppose Mordley came from, looks French and Scots mixed. Say he was anything up to fifty when Dugald was born. What important events happened in the fifty years before 1835 in France? "

Ross smiled wryly. " I'm not very well up in French history," he confessed, picking up the hammer. " I only know one date. 1789, the French — "

" What? " said Holly hopefully.

" The French Revolution," Ross grinned.

They both burst out laughing.

" Of course! He must have been born around 1789," Holly said. " But it's no good writing to Aunt Lottie. I don't think she'd go to Paris for us, because she can't speak French, and in any case she disapproves of Paris. Ross, I've just thought of something. If Revolution was the Old Villain's son and he was born in France, then the Old Villain must have been in France too. We left him on Trillsean. What's he doing in France and giving his son a defiant name like Revolution? "

" Come to the cookhouse door, boys," yelled Pud, staggering out with the tray.

" We'll have another dig at it later," Ross said, taking the tray and gazing approvingly at the sausages and onions.

But it was half past ten before they had another chance to talk. The Commander had rehearsed them solidly all the evening and then sent them to bed with strict instructions not to gossip. Pud unwound her plaits and was counting gloomily as she brushed her hair.

" Forty-nine, fifty. I don't know why I do this every night. It never seems to look any better. I do wish I wasn't plain. Though I met an awfully nice man who didn't seem to mind."

" Tell me," Holly said eagerly, wriggling into her sleeping bag. " Ross and I have been so busy talking about ourselves, we haven't even asked you if you've had any fun."

" Nothing much," Pud admitted. " Sixty-two, sixty-three. We hadn't a thing to eat for dinner one day at Fort Augustus, so I went fishing in Loch Ness. I'd caught a couple of trout right off when I saw this man watching me kind of enviously. Well, you know me. I'll talk to anybody. He said he was a policeman. Gosh, he wasn't a bit like my idea of a policeman. Quite old, of course, at least forty. But very attracted by me, all the same."

Here Pud put down the brush and tired to drape herself elegantly against the soapbox which served her for a dressing table.

" He was out fishing for his dinner too. So I slipped the trout into his basket."

" Go on," Holly said eagerly. " What else happened? "

" He's got a beautiful fast launch and took me for a ride — I mean, a cruise down Loch Ness."

Pud tried to yawn languidly and give the impression that she was extremly tired of all the men who kept thrusting launch trips upon her. She leaned more heavily upon the soapbox, which promptly gave way and sent her crashing onto the ground sheet. Holly shrieked with laughter and picked her up. Pud grinned, set the dressing table up on end again, and picked up the hairbrush.

" Oh, well," she sighed, " what was I saying? Oh, yes, we had this glorious trip and he showed me the trees he sat in."

" What does he sit in trees for? " Holly demanded. " On the lookout for criminals or something? "

" No," Pud said, " birds. He's mad on birds and makes hidey-holes for himself in trees and goes and peers at them through a telescope or something. I had a whale of a time, really. And what do you think? He's at Fort William and saw our show! Eighty-nine, ninety."

" He sounds most intriguing. We'll simply have to look out for him when we do our Scottish legends program," Holly declared.

" He said he starts some leave in a few days and when — "

" Listen, that's Ross shouting," Holly broke in. " He sounds as if he's bursting with excitement. Can he come in? "

Pud nodded. " Ninety-seven, ninety-eight."

" Come in, Ross, and get it off your chest," Holly called.

Ross threw back the tent flap.

" Just a minute," Pud said. " Ninety-nine, a hundred."

She laid the brush down. " All right. Go on, Ross. I've got a bottle of lemonade somewhere. If you don't mind drinking out of a jam jar. I can't sneak a cup because Aunt Caroline doesn't know I've got it. She says it's bad for my figure."

" And I've found some cold sausages in the Globe," Ross said, laying a dish containing three sausages on the end of Holly's sleeping bag. " Listen. I was deep in my daily grind at this unearthly language and thought I'd try to translate ' He must not blow the Lantern out ' into Gaelic just to see how I was getting on. I found I could do it all except ' Lantern,' so I looked it up in the dictionary."

" Yes? " said Holly, sitting up.

" See for yourself," Ross replied. " Here by my finger."

Holly drew the hurricane lamp nearer and bent over the book.

" Trillsean," she whispered.

They stared into each other's eyes.

" No wonder Mad Mollie talked about the Lantern as if it was a very special thing. She must have meant the island," Holly murmured.

" Do you think so? " Ross said doubtfully. " I gathered she spoke of the Lantern as if it were a person. Not a thing. You don't call an island ' him.' "

14

AS HANDSOME A VILLAIN

It was the last night of their Inverness week. Pud stood in front of the mirror in the Moray Hall dressing room trying to fix her black-velvet page-boy hat at a becoming angle over her sandy plaits.

"Do you know," she complained to Holly, "I've put this thing on a different way every night this week and not one of them's looked right. The Commander says you've got to convince the audience you really are the person you're acting. I don't believe I've hoodwinked our audiences once this week. I'll just bet they know it's fat, freckled Pauline Broome-Gilson all the time. It's my face that's the trouble. Freckles and feathers just don't mix."

Holly grinned sympathetically. "Try some of that heavy peach base. And then powder heavily over it."

She picked up the air cushion and began inflating it, ready for Major Lumley.

"I'm scared stiff of this stage-managing," she confessed. "Ross says he won't help me tonight and I've got to do it all on my own. I'm sure something will go wrong."

"Nothing ever does," Pud said. She anchored the hat with a large hatpin and surveyed the result gloomily. "You do the footsteps-coming-up-stairs bit with those two pieces of wood, and the door knocker with the two pound-weights and the sound of Catherine Parr making her pastry by banging the pillow on the floor. And when the king calls for musicians you start the portable with 'Greensleeves.' And tie the king's stomach on tight so it doesn't drop off."

"All right," Holly sighed. "I'll do my best. Where's the script? I'll have to prompt as well."

She lifted her pearl and lace headdress and laid it carefully over her curly hair.

Pud sighed. "Catherine of Aragon, you're wonderful. Every inch a queen. And Ross looks more dashing than ever in that plumed hat. Oh, well, come on. Curtain's due up in a couple of minutes."

The Moray Hall was full. Once again Holly experienced that moment when she waited in the wings for the signal and heard that hush sink over the audience as the curtains parted.

And once again all her fears left her directly she had spoken her opening words. Her scene with Ross as the ardent young king in love for the first time received its usual heartening ovation.

She removed her headdress and slipped out of the sky-blue embroidered dress and ruff. Scene two of *A King's Conversation Piece* was about to begin. Major Lumley waddled to the wings with her.

"Your Order of the Garter's on the wrong leg," hissed Catherine Parr, alias the Commander, in a stern whisper. "Too late! You're on."

Pud had opened the next scene. Her voice, which always seemed to rise at least an octave when she was playing a part, squeaked out the cue. The Major, lost in a frantic effort to change his Garter, missed it.

With great presence of mind, Pud strolled around the

back of the stage chair and spoke the line again.

Henry the Eighth shot on suddenly from the wings, propelled by a vigorous push from Catherine Parr. The audience received him with a howl of delight. The more the poor Major stammered and tried to regain his self-control, the more entangled he became.

On swept Catherine Parr at the right cue. The anxiety of hearing the scene being played out of step caused her to take her part at a tremendous pace and further embarrass the hapless Major. He could hardly gasp out his lines in the violent stage quarrel between the king and his domineering last wife. The Commander, as she usually did off stage, got the better of it.

Ross heard the gales of laughter and flew out to join Holly in the wings.

" What's going on? " he whispered. " They don't usually howl like this, do they? "

Holly, tears of merriment running down over her make-up, tried to tell him. Ross took one glance at the stage and began shaking too. And then he took a second glance, swallowed hard and whistled under his breath.

" Henry's stomach. It's collapsing! "

Holly's face sobered. She clapped a hand over her mouth.

" I thought I heard a hissing noise in between the laughs. Perhaps I didn't tighten the valve enough. Poor Major, this'll finish him off completely."

" He's got a short exit in a minute," Ross whispered urgently. " Get ready to blow him up."

They saw the dejected king stumble across the stage, followed by a last triumphant shaft from Catherine Parr.

" Grab him," Ross muttered. " I'll blow him up. You get ready for the door-knock cue."

" Over here quick," Ross hissed. " I want you."

The Major's face, already hot and flurried, dropped still farther.

" What's wrong now, my dear fella? I got a clap."

" You're fine," Ross grinned. " It's just your stomach. It's losing its grip."

The Major, with a dismayed grimace, clapped both hands to the air cushion. With a heart-rending " wheeeee " which rose to the roof of the Moray Hall it gave up the last of its air.

" Knocker cue," gasped Ross to Holly. " Quick! He's on again. No time to pump him up. Give me that pillow."

He ripped off the tapes and stuffed the pillow up under Henry the Eighth's tunic.

" You'll just have to hold it on, Major. There's your cue. Don't let go, for Pete's sake." He turned to Holly. " Wake up. There's the footsteps cue. Quick! "

Holly, hot and breathless, grabbed the two pieces of wood and pushed them at Ross.

" You do it," she begged. " I can't keep pace with this stage-managing."

The audience clapped for a solid five minutes when the curtain swished together. The Major had to take half a dozen bows, and even then the audience were reluctant to let him go.

Holly fell on Pud as she left the stage. " Here! — I thought you said nothing ever happened! It's been frightful. No more stage-managing for me. I'm hopeless."

But as usual Holly wasn't hopeless at holding the audience in perfect silence while she sang. The three-piece orchestra faded from " Weel May the Keel Row " into " Charlie Is My Darling." Holly took a step forward and held out her hands over the footlights. They thundered out the chorus, drowning both her and the three-piece.

She took her tumultuous applause with her usual bow, sent a happy smile over their heads, and looked straight into the eyes of Murdo Dundas standing at the back.

Holly dashed off the stage, dodged the Commander, who was just about to begin one of her comedy sketches, and found Ross.

" Guess who's propping up the exit door? " she panted.

" Deathshead, our most ardent admirer," Ross said, pulling off his beard.

" Right first go. What's he doing in Inverness? It's miles from Inverkenneth. Doesn't he ever do any work? "

" Got the sack, perhaps, or given up his job."

Holly laughed a little nervously.

" Seriously, Holly, I mean it. I believe whatever's on his mind is so important to him now that he would give up his job for it. I'm not a bit surprised he's appeared in Inverness."

" But why? " Holly faltered.

" Because we're here," Ross rejoined.

" Are we going to look astonished to see him or what? " Holly went on.

" We're going to look innocently delighted to renew his acquaintance. And if we find him trailing us, we're going to pretend we don't know anything about it," Ross said firmly, opening the side door. " He's nowhere in sight at the moment. And it's raining."

" Raining? " Holly echoed. " It's impossible for it to be raining. It was fine when we came in."

" Well, it is. Look." Ross flicked a handful of raindrops over her.

Holly groaned. " What a country! It never does anything but rain. Tomorrow's Saturday too. We were going to have a free week end before going back to Fort

William. I wanted to go up to Culloden and have a look at the headstones to see if I could get any more information on the Old Villain."

"He wouldn't have fought at Culloden. He'd have been too young or not even born," Ross remarked.

"I know," Holly said, "but I thought perhaps his father might have been there fighting for Prince Charles Stuart and that's how his estate got given to Lowland Scots. All the estates of Highlanders who fought for the prince got confiscated and given to people who supported the English."

"I see," Ross said. "Well, perhaps it'll be fine tomorrow."

It wasn't fine. It poured all night and gusts of chilly rain still blew about in the wind the next morning.

Holly, peeling the potatoes for dinner, stared at the broad back of the Commander, who was sewing furiously.

"What are you making, Mrs. Lumley?" she asked idly, watching the rain lash against the windows of the Globe. "Is it something for the Scottish legends program?"

"It is," replied the Commander. "Bumble, what does a Highland bonnet look like? I must have some idea if I'm to make Ross one for the chieftain's costume. Wake up, Bumble, don't just sit there and look helpless."

The Major shook his head forlornly. "I don't know, my dear. We wore caps in the Royal Engineers. It's still raining."

"I'm not talking about the Royal Engineers!" snapped the Commander. "I'm talking about Highland bonnets. And don't keep grumbling about the rain."

"If it's a bonnet pattern you want," stammered the Major, "I suppose — suppose it would look — like a bonnet."

The Commander treated him to an icy stare.

"I mean, a lady's bonnet," he put in hastily," with a—feather—and things."

"Ladies' bonnets went out with my grandmother," the Commander replied grimly. "The trouble with you, Bumble, is that you're a hundred years behind the times."

"Surely not, my dear," protested the Major meekly. "Not quite a hundred surely. The rain's made you a little irritable."

"The rain has nothing to do with it and I am not in the least irritable," she returned. "Holly and Ross will have to put on their raincoats and visit the museum this afternoon."

Holly let the last potato fall with a splash into the water.

"Oh, must we?" she groaned. "A museum—on a Saturday!"

"You'll enjoy it," the Commander nodded. "A nice instructive afternoon. It has a fine collection of tartans and some interesting spinning wheels, I believe."

Holly pulled a dismal face. "Spinning wheels! I suppose there are stuffed birds and bits of flint in dusty cases as well."

"Doubtless," beamed the Commander. "All museums have stuffed birds and bits of flint. You will both find it most amusing, and if there is no picture of a Highland bonnet, you can make some inquiries."

Ross and Holly set out after dinner was over, heads down to the slashing rain.

"Enjoy yourselves," the Commander called brightly after them. "And don't come back without a picture of a Highland bonnet."

"I'm sure I saw a dear familiar figure's hat walking

along behind us in the crowd as we came past the Harris tweed shop," Holly murmured, stripping the paper off a bar of chocolate.

" So did I," Ross replied. " But these two little innocents have simply no idea he's trailing us. Serve him right if he lands up among the glass cases."

The museum didn't turn out so badly after all. It was empty except for a dried-up little man asleep under a newspaper in the Battle of Culloden room.

" It's warm and dry, anyway," Holly said. " Look, Ross. It says all these things were found on the battlefield."

" And here's a collection of six stones used by a witch when making spells. It's really true, then. I thought perhaps you and Hurdie were pulling my leg," Ross remarked.

So engrossed were they that they entirely forgot both Murdo Dundas and the Highland bonnet.

The little dry man had awakened at the sound of their eager voices.

" 'Tis braw tae see th' young interesting themsel' in th' auld," he observed, his apple cheeks creasing into a network of smiling lines.

" It's all rather exciting. We thought we'd be bored. Ross, the Highland bonnet! Perhaps he'll know," she whispered, nodding toward the seat. The dry man noticed her hesitant glance.

" Enoch Bunker, my dear," he said, getting up stiffly. " Known locally as Bunker's Books. D'ye wish for some information? I always come here on a Saturday, oot of th' hurry o' th' crowds daein' their messages. I like th' feel of th' past."

" We want to track down a Highland bonnet," Holly said. " There isn't a picture of one here, I suppose? "

" Hae ye visited the tartans? " inquired Mr. Bunker.

" N-no," Holly said. " We thought they would be dull."

" Tut-tut. Dull? Ye come wi' me. Now here's a Hieland Blue Bonnet. 'Twas dug oot of a peat bog near Garve in 1935."

" But it's green," smiled Ross. " Or is that what they call blue in these parts? "

" Nae, 'tis a blue bonnet but th' lang lie in th' peat has turned it tae th' green. There's the slit in th' side whaur th' mon would put his clan emblem. Heath for MacDonalds, boxwood for th' MacKintosh clan, and so on."

Holly stared at the bonnet, and then at Ross. " That's where the Old Villain would have put his bunch of white roses," she said. " Pity Mother isn't here. She would have drawn us a lovely picture of it for the Commander. I'll have to see what I can do on this chocolate paper. Are there any oil paintings or portraits here, Mr. Bunker? I always have to keep a lookout for my mother. She's batty on portraits, especially Raeburns."

Mr. Bunker shook his head. " They hae a fine Van Dyck in th' museum, but most of th' Raeburns are in Edinburgh. Though judging by a letter frae th' great Raeburn himsel', there's one o' his paintings that's lost tae an admirin' world."

" How can a Raeburn have got lost? " asked Holly. " It would be worth thousands now, wouldn't it? "

" Naebody kens, lass. I buy up th' odd lots of auld books for ma shop. I hae piles o' them and it got so that I couldna move. I'm sortin' them oot when these letters fa' frae an auld tattered book o' Scottish pictures. Maybe they'd be worth a heap o' money but I canna bear tae be parted frae th' beauties. One's frae a cousin o' David Deuchar to David Deuchar himsel' and other's frae th' great Raeburn tae this cousin in London."

"About this missing picture, you mean?" put in Ross.

"And whose picture was it? You don't know, I suppose," Holly added.

"'Twas o' some auld swashbuklin' laddie that Raeburn went tae school with. Seemingly frae th' letters th' master was gey fond o' this laddie. Could ye drink some tea and eat a bannock?" Mr. Bunker added suddenly.

"Rather!" Ross and Holly replied eagerly.

"Ye come along wi' me. I've only got a wee room ower th' shop but ye're welcome. I'll show ye th' letters."

Enoch Bunker's room was indeed wee and, to add to the smallness, it was crammed from floor to ceiling with an incredible collection of old swords, warming pans, statues, and, where there was a square inch of space between them, with books of every shape and degree of antiquity.

"This is ma stock room," he announced, hopping between the obstructions.

"I thought you said you'd only got one room," Holly exclaimed.

"Aye, only th' one room," beamed Mr. Bunker.

"Then — where do you sleep?" Holly said.

"In ma stock room."

"And have your meals?" put in Ross.

"In th' stock room," repeated Mr. Bunker, nodding. I hae th' wee oilstove." He lifted a pompous-faced marble bust to reveal the oilstove nestling in the hollow underneath. "I'm short of th' space. I hae to tak' care o' every inch. And I canna lose ma oilstove if I ken Sir Jacob's takin' care o' it."

"And your — bed?" Holly stammered.

"Ma bed? Aye, I hae a braw bed, but I canna show it tae ye. 'Tis behind th' wee pile o' books. When I hae ma supper, I tak' doon th' books for ma table an' there is ma bed all ready for me tae rest in! "

Holly shook her head and smiled. " I can see you need someone to take care of you, Mr. Bunker."

An expression of deepest alarm flitted over the old man's withered-apple face. " Ye mean a — wifie? I'm nea needin' a wifie. She's be richt fashed at ma stock room and in would come th' brooms an' pails an' ma comfort's awa' for aye. Can ye see ma kettle, bairns? I'm needin' tae make ye th' tea. Dinna fash yersen. . . . I may hae tae'n it doon tae th' shop. I'll flit an' see, an' ye can read th' letters whiles I'm lookin'."

He picked his way over to a warming pan and removed two yellow papers from under the lid. " They're safe in th' pan," he explained. " Touch 'em wi' gentle hands, lass. They're richt auld an' precious tae me. This is th' first one t'read. I need tae tell ye this David Deuchar th' cousin writes tae is th' David Deuchar who was a seal engraver. Th' great Raeburn when but a wee lad of fourteen or so was apprenticed tae a goldsmith by name o' James Gilliland and this David Deuchar did business wi' th' goldsmith. He maun hae been a verra auld mon when this correspondence took place. Read th' letter frae th' cousin tae David Deuchar firrst. He maun hae showed it tae Raeburn, as th' second letter is frae Raeburn tae th' cousin livin' in London."

Mr. Bunker laid the letters reverently in Holly's hands and shuffled out and down the narrow stair to the shop.

" '*From Samuel Kilbride, clerk to my Lord's Commissioners at the Admiralty, to his cousin David Deuchar in Edinburgh, December, 1805,*' " Holly read. " Let's go a bit nearer what's left of the window, Ross. The ink's very faded. Perhaps we could move a few of these books down and sit on them. Museums are hard on the feet."

They piled the books on the floor and leaned against the wall.

"Just a minute," Ross said. "Let me take this statue's arm out of my shoulder blades. All right. I'm reasonably comfortable if you are. Fire away."

"'*My dear cousin,*'" Holly began. "'*I hope you continue in the best of health apart from those infirmities which the hand of time lays upon us all.*

"'*I write to acquaint you of an item of news which may interest your famous acquaintance Sir Henry Raeburn. I have come, in the lamentable list of casualties incidental to our glorious victory at Trafalgar, upon the name of one Fireflaught, who, if my memory serves me aright, was a friend of your illustrious fellow countryman. I am distressed to acquaint you of the fact, however, that the said Fireflaught did not die under the command of our immortal Lord Nelson, God rest his soul, but in the service of the hated French flag. His body was found on the quarterdeck of* H.M.S. Agamemnon, *he having evidently boarded the ship to carry his hatred of our noble country to closer quarters.*

"'*I grieve to impart to so zealous a Scot as yourself the defection of a fellow Scot, but I feel Sir Henry would wish to know the ignoble fate of his erstwhile friend.*

"'*Much as I deplore the renegade act of the said Fireflaught, nevertheless from all reports he appears to have fought with great bravery until receiving the fatal thrust.*

"'*If your friend Raeburn would be so good I should be indebted to hear a little of this man's history that I may be the less at a loss to account for his miserable treachery in furthering the cause of the accursed Bonaparte. Your devoted cousin-in-law, Samuel Kilbride.*'"

Holly folded the paper into its worn creases. Ross was staring thoughtfully at the dusty floor.

" Here's another Scot fighting for the French like our Revolution Ross. It seemed quite the fashion."

Holly stared at him. " I wonder — if this Fireflaught could have had anything to do with Revolution Ross! "

Ross shook his head. " No, the name's quite different."

" Of course it is. What a pity! It would have been a marvelous bit of luck, wouldn't it? "

" Get on to Sir Henry Raeburn's letter," Ross suggested. " I'm getting quite interested in poor old Fireflaught and Mr. Samuel Kilbride's low opinion of him."

Holly unfolded the long, delicately written letter, the beauty of its lettering still visible on the faded paper.

" '*Sir Henry Raeburn, Edinburgh, to Mr. Samuel Kilbride of London, February, 1806. Dear Sir, the esteemed friend of my first master, the honest James Gilliland, namely, Mr. David Deuchar, having only lately recovered from an attack of ague, has shown me your letter to him concerning my dear acquaintance Fireflaught.*

" '*I grieve exceedingly at your sad news and cannot find it in my heart to condemn him as you, sir, are apparently able to do, for we are commanded in Holy Writ that we judge not, lest we be judged.*

" '*We were boys together at Heriot's Hospital here in Edinburgh and were apprenticed into the world together, he to a jeweler to acquire the art of cutting and polishing precious stones under the shadow of St. Giles and I to the afore-mentioned James Gilliland.*

" '*He was a fearless boy, always to the fore in any sort of affray, though never in my life did I receive aught but kindness from him, he having the native nobility of the lion with the innocent trusting heart of the lamb, a nature quick to burst aflame and yet as quick to take a hurt. Even as a boy he evinced an impatience of authority and in truth I can but honestly tell you, sir, that all through his life he was a wanted man in greater or lesser degree. For, his father having lost his estate after Culloden, Fireflaught took to the sea and continued to wear the forbidden Highland dress. He even, I believe, continued to live, a hunted man, on a portion of the old family estate, the new inhabitants being so afeared of him they could not prevent it.*

" '*For years he was lost to me until one night there came a knock on the door of my studio in George Street and in strode Fireflaught in the full Highland dress of clan chieftain, a keg of brandy for me on his shoulder. I made haste to pull him within for fear of his life and he lay hidden with me some fourteen days.*

" '*So struck was I with his appearance, he being then at the age of thirty-two years and in the full beauty of his manhood, that I did do a portrait of him in his clan dress, with his full titles below, as handsome a villain as ever wore an eagle's feather in his bonnet. Hardly was the paint dry on the canvas but he was off with the portrait wrapped in a sack.*

" '*I never saw him again and never heard the rights of it, but 'twas noised abroad he had been betrayed to the revenue officers and after a furious battle at sea taken south for hanging.*

" '*I rejoice to hear from your letter that he died a braver death than hanging and I rejoice also, sir, that he should have escaped the English, even though the wound of betrayal by his fellow countrymen should have caused him to fight for her enemies.*

" '*I never hope to meet a better man this side of Paradise, as God is my judge, and when you, sir, come to the judgment seat, may your sins be forgiven you as readily, I confidently believe, as will his. I am, sir, your obedient servant, Henry Raeburn.'* "

Holly was silent, looking down at the letter which still seemed to glow with the burning spirit of a man roused in defense of his friend.

Ross put his hands into his pockets and smiled grimly.

" I'll bet that thundering denunciation of all mealy-mouthed hypocrites put the pompous Samuel Kilbride in his place! "

" I wish I'd know Sir Henry Raeburn," Holly said thoughtfully. " He was a true friend and a fearless one. And this Fireflaught too. How could anyone sink so low as to betray a man like that, whatever he'd done? "

Holly got to her feet, an indignant flush on her face.

" The Samuel Kilbrides and Murdo Dundases of this world are always ready to sell their souls for a nice fat recompense," Ross remarked.

" And why, oh, why didn't Raeburn mention the titles in his letter! And where's the picture? "

" Do you know something, Holly? " Ross said suddenly. " I reckon the Old Villain might have been one of Fireflaught's men. He must have had a crew."

Holly caught her breath. " What makes you think so? Because of the mention of France? "

" Partly. There are one or two curious bits in that letter which seem to match up with what little we know of the Old Villain. It's the same period exactly. There's the life at sea and the keg of brandy, smuggled no doubt, and Fireflaught knowing how to cut and polish stones. He must have been a great friend of the Old Villain's to do that for him. If it was he who did it, of course. Though it seems a pretty likely possibility. Then there's the enlistment in the

French Navy. Revolution Ross was apparently in the French Army if he was killed at Strasbourg in 1836."

Holly bit her lip. "You mean Fireflaught and Ross E escaped somehow and got to France."

Ross nodded. "And Fireflaught was killed at Trafalgar and Ross E married and had a son."

"And the Macaudré bit got tacked on in France. Where Mordley came from, I expect," added Holly. "Oh, I do so hope Ross E was one of Fireflaught's men. If only he had known Fireflaught, it would be something. To think we possessed even that little bit of him! I wonder what happened to the rest of the crew."

"They were probably mostly fellow clansmen and all got wiped out in the sea battle. It would be a fight to the death with men like that."

Holly sighed. "Poor fellows. Let's put the letters back. Here's Mr. Bunker struggling up the stairs and, by the sound of it, he's traced the kettle."

15

THE EAGLE FEATHERS

Ross and Holly, full of tea and bannocks, bore the chocolate wrapper back to the Globe in triumph.

" It's broad and flat, like this, knitted from wool and a dark-blue color," Holly panted. "You wear it tilted to one side and there's a slit in it to take the clan emblem. And if it belongs to the chief, the eagle's feathers as well."

The Commander beamed approvingly. " Very good work. It couldn't have been as dull as you thought, you've been so long. We've had tea."

" And been down to the town and bought up a box of kippers," Pud said. " We've got a visitor for supper."

" He called this afternoon and I thought Ross and Holly would be so glad to see him again," the Commander put in briskly.

" Who? Someone exciting? " Holly asked.

" That nice Mr. Dundas we met at Inverkenneth. He's been here for hours and talking about you all the time. He wanted to know everything you've been doing. Just fancy him being in Inverness. What a coincidence! "

" Just fancy! " Ross murmured. " I'm looking forward to renewing our unpleasant acquaintance."

" You two and Pud'll have to cook the kippers. I must

get on with this Highland bonnet. Where's that old blue knitted jumper of mine? Dear me! "

The Commander's ample bosom heaved in agitation. " We've got no eagle feathers! "

The Major lowered his copy of the *Racing News*. "It won't matter, my dear. I'll run out tomorrow and find you some other bird's feathers. They'll do fine."

The Commander fixed him with a stony stare. " They will not do fine, Bumble," she said. " You've been in the theatrical business with me long enough to know I will not tolerate the second best. It's an eagle feather or nothing. If there's no eagle feather, there's no clan chieftain in the show."

" But it'll ruin it to take him out," Holly protested.

" Better to do that than have makeshifts," the Commander replied firmly, and made a great cut in the blue jumper.

" Where are we going to get an eagle feather? " Holly exclaimed. " Eagles are rare birds."

" Perhaps the Commander could ask that nice Mr. Dundas," Ross suggested. " He's always so anxious to help."

Holly grinned and hung her raincoat up to dry over the stove.

The pile of kippers leaned precariously over the hot plate like a succulent Tower of Pisa when Dundas entered the cozy, overcrowded, happy atmosphere of the Globe. Like a nasty shower at a picnic, Holly thought grimly. She felt tempted to give him one or two of the thin, stringy fish she had found at the bottom of the box, but, remembering her father's stern rules about Scottish hospitality, she regretfully handed him the four juiciest she could find.

The Commander, determined to get an eagle feather from somewhere, led the conversation skillfully around from some rare fossils she had found in Dorset to bird sanctuaries and on to golden eagles.

"And have you ever seen one, Mr. Dundas? We require one of their feathers," she said. "Let me take your bones away."

Dundas stared at her a moment, then, seeing her hand held out, gave her his plate.

"Many times," he said. "There's an old nest on the northeast face of Ben Nevis. I was up there in April and saw two eggs."

"Ben Nevis!" Holly exclaimed. "Could we climb it?"

A ray of light passed through the impenetrable darkness of Dundas' eyes.

"Certainly you could." He glanced briefly at Ross. "Though no doubt you would choose the soft, easy route the trippers take."

Ross flushed. "We'd go the stiffest way possible for people who aren't — rock-climbers," he replied, tossing his head back in a haughty gesture Holly had never seen before.

"Good." Dundas' brooding face became almost animated.

"It looks as if we shall have our eagle feathers after all," the Commander beamed, as she left the Globe with the discarded bones.

"Where shall I meet you?" Dundas went on easily, showing his even white teeth.

"Nowhere," retorted Ross. "We aren't coming."

With his head thrown back, he stared down at Dundas, his face stern and contemptuous.

Pud and the Major looked on with open mouths. Holly instinctively drew closer to Ross.

A dull, red glow of anger spread over Dundas' forehead.

With his powerful hands clenched, he glared across the table.

"You haughty Highlander," he muttered. "Step carefully and be civil." He dropped his voice to a breath. "Or you too shall suffer at the hand of a Dundas. Are you coming or not?"

Holly felt Ross stiffen.

"You — betrayer," he whispered. "Find some other way this time."

"Coward," breathed Dundas softly.

Ross sprang up. The teacups went crashing to the floor. He lashed forward with his arm and hit Dundas a heavy blow on the forehead.

The Commander, re-entering the Globe, stopped transfixed.

"Ross!" she cried sharply. "Are you mad? Mr. Dundas is our guest. You will apologize at once."

"I will not," Ross snarled. "No one calls me that without suffering for it. Tell him to get out before I land him another crack."

The Commander's lips tightened.

Dundas rose and bowed to her. "I regret my offer has not been welcome. I was only hoping to assist you to find your eagle feathers. Now I fear you will have to look elsewhere. Good night."

He replaced his chair and went out, closing the door softly behind him.

The Commander looked sternly at Ross. "Have you anything to say, young man?"

Ross got up and put on his jacket. "No," he said.

"Then I suggest you go straight to bed," the Commander replied quietly.

Ross nodded and left the Globe. Holly burst into tears

and started to follow him. The Commander put out her hand.

" Let him alone to cool off," she said. " He must have taken leave of his senses."

" It's not that at all," Holly sobbed. " You don't understand. You don't know what it's about, Mrs. Lumley. Dundas — he — Ross will have to tell you."

The journey back to Fort William the next day took place in melancholy silence. In silence they had their dinner at the old camping site by the military road. Ross buried himself in his Gaelic textbook. Holly took to pressing flowers, an activity the Commander viewed with no little private astonishment. Pud made several mysterious trips to the town and returned each time with little appetite for meals.

At last Holly could bear it no longer. She went over and, sitting down beside Ross, put her arm through his. " Let's tell the Commander everything," she begged.

Ross pressed her hand. " She won't believe us. She likes Dundas. And I'm not keen on telling tales behind people's backs."

" We told Daddy and he believed us."

" That was different. He had to be told because you belong to him. It's different with me. I paddle my own canoe," he added grimly.

Holly bit her lip. " Don't say it like that. You know you belong to us and we care what happens to you. The Commander's very sweet, really. She'll believe you."

" All right," Ross said, getting up. They trailed over to the Globe and knocked on the door.

" Come in," the Commander said. " Well, my dears? "

Ross stood in front of her and put his hands in his pockets.

" I know you like Dundas, Mrs. Lumley, and I don't want to appear to be saying nasty things behind his back. But — Besides, I don't know whether you'll believe me."

The Commander, her handsome face pale and unhappy, motioned to them to sit down.

" Why should I not believe you? I've never found you anything but perfectly honest and truthful."

" It's not quite that. It's perhaps too — fantastic to swallow," Ross said. " But I'll tell you just the same."

He clasped his hands and told her the whole story behind the ducking in Loch Kennth and the terrible trip through Corrievreckan.

The Commander listened in silence, her direct eyes on his face.

" And he was the man who left the show in such a hurry? Why in the name of goodness didn't you tell me all this before? The wretched creature. To think we gave him the four best kippers."

Holly burst into tears. " Mrs. Lumley, you're an angel," she faltered. " We thought you were so cross because — because we wouldn't trouble to go after the eagle feathers."

" I don't like things like this coming between me and my children," the Commander faltered in return. " And what is his next move going to be? I shan't feel satisfied now I've heard all this unless you are both well and truly tethered where I can see you."

Holly laughed in the middle of her tears and ended up by choking. Ross was clapping her vigorously on the back when Pud burst in.

" Just been to post office. Wire for Holly. Can't stop. Coffee with a man."

" I am giving an interview, Pauline," the Commander began majestically. But Pud had already gone.

They looked at each other in astonishment and all three burst out laughing.

" It's coming to something." The Commander tried to speak severely. " Coffee with a man, indeed! "

" It's probably that policeman she told me about," Holly grinned.

" In that case, she's in safe hands," Ross remarked. " Who sent the wire? " I wish someone would write to me."

" It's Daddy," Holly said. " He's rather a lamb. Listen! ' HAVEN'T SEEN YOU FOR AGES STOP ARE YOU STILL ALIVE STOP HAVE FORGOTTEN WHAT YOU LOOK LIKE STOP CAN YOU SPARE FEW DAYS CHEER OUR OLD AGE STOP LOVE LONELY PARENTS.' Isn't he funny? I ought to have written. I do believe he's taken to sending wires just to frighten poor Miss Ethnie."

The Commander's normal urbanity had returned. " I think we can accede to his request, dear child," she said graciously. " I was about to tell you when my niece's outburst put me off. A little reward because Holly's been such a good trouper. We take the show to Fluran tomorrow."

Holly gasped joyfully. " Mrs. Lumley, you're an — "

" I know! Don't tell me. I'm an angel. You can go and wire your poor father the Globe Players will descend upon him at about midday Thursday. We'll take our own food to save embarrassing your mother."

" How — how are we all going to get there? " stammered Holly. " *Sea Rider* will take part of us. What about the rest? And the costumes and so on? "

" I shall hire a boat," the Commander replied, " and live on bread and water through the winter. The post office is ten minutes' walk. I shall expect you both back here in twenty minutes."

Ross and Holly were back in nineteen and a half minutes, though they had been tempted to linger by an intriguing glimpse of Pud chatting with a smart young policeman at the window table of Fort William's most select teashop.

They were sitting around and about to attack a blackberry tart, the fruit for which Holly had picked during her flower-pressing period, when Pud staggered up the slope.

" You're late," announced the Commander. " There's hardly anything left."

" I don't care," Pud groaned. " I'm not hungry."

" Pud not hungry? " they all exclaimed in astonishment.

" She's ill," Ross added with mock alarm.

" I'm not. I'm full of doughnuts," Pud replied.

" How many? " Ross inquired with a wicked grin. " And with whom? "

" About half a crown's worth. With Sergeant Dryden. I was out with him this morning. Mr. Tarbet's told all the police about me and they all want to take me out. I said they'd have to take it in turns."

Pud leaned back languidly and sighed. Ross grinned with delight.

" It's terrible being so popular, isn't it? " he murmured.

The Commander clicked her teeth. " Oh, Pud, and with your figure too. You'll end your days as a fat woman in a circus, you mark my words."

" No, I won't," Pud retorted. " I'm going on a diet. Will you lend me your white jumper and that silk scarf of yours, Holly? "

" Of course I will," Holly said. " And my white beads too, if you like."

" Going out again already? " Ross added, pointedly removing her blackberry tart and putting down a dry piece of bread.

" If you must be so inquisitive, Mr. Mordley," remarked Pud with dignity, " I'm going out to tea."

" With the same policeman? " Ross exclaimed.

" No, another one." And Pud caught him neatly over the head with the empty pie dish.

They were having a furious cribbage battle when Pud once more burst in late the same evening.

" Here are your eagle feathers. Hugh picked them out of a stuffed eagle in his second-best bedroom. And I've got you a crowd of villages too," she added, panting and laying a pound box of chocolates down across the playing cards.

" You've what? " inquired the Commander, inspecting her over the top of her reading glasses.

" Got you a crowd of villagers. Hugh's just starting his other week's leave and says he'll come and do the villagers for us. And you needn't hire a boat, because he'll come in his and cart the stuff over for you."

Pud leaned against the door to recover her breath.

The Commander shook her head dubiously. " Sit down and collect your scattered wits, Pauline. First of all, what does ' cart the stuff ' mean and who is Hugh? If you mean Mr. Tarbet, I do feel — "

" Aunt Caroline," Pud began firmly. " You simply can't go out with a man and call him Mr. Something. It destroys all the romance."

" Oh, it does, does it? " the Commander replied with considerable astonishment. " I understood he was old enough to be your father. In my young days, little girls — "

" But that's ages ago, Aunt Caroline," protested Pud. " And he insists. He's going to have me for his mascot. He's got a beautiful launch. He sold it to some Americans but they messed it up terribly and he couldn't bear it, so he's just bought it back. He's — he's renaming her the *Pauline*."

The Commander digested this information. " He sounds most unlike a member of the constabulary."

" His father left him a lot of money," Pud said, opening the box of chocolates and staring thoughtfully at the contents. " He's told me the story of his life. He's not very keen on money. But he simply adores crime. So he joined the police."

The Commander choked slightly. Holly burst out laughing and in a moment Pud's audience was shrieking with merriment. Pud carefully picked out a hard center from the chocolates and put it in her mouth, a dubious smile on her simple, freckled face.

" What did I say funny? " she inquired, watching them.

16

LANTERN OF THE NORTH

EARLY the next morning Ross and Holly, loaded with stores and equipment, arrived at the Fort William pier.

"Do you see what I see?" she exclaimed. "Look! The launch from Oban."

"Formerly the *Peek-a-Boo,* I believe," Ross grinned. "And with the toast of the Fort William police force on board too."

"Pud? Where?" Holly demanded. "It must be Mr. Tarbet's boat."

"Ahoy there!" yelled Pud, brandishing a fishing rod. Ross and Holly moved forward and stood staring down at the launch.

A good-looking, rugged man who had been bending over the compass glanced up at them. They jumped down and Pud introduced them.

"I like your ship," Ross observed, looking around.

Tarbet smiled ruefully. "Her heart's still in the right place in spite of her somewhat frivolous exterior. I'm itching to scrape that stuff off and get her back to her original white paint and varnish."

"Basil," Pud remarked to Sergeant Dryden, "there's the Commander. Give her a hand, will you?"

Ross glanced at Holly, who grinned delightedly.

The Commander eyed *Sea Rider,* which lay bobbing alongside the *Pauline.*

" I think I'd better travel with Mr. Tarbet," she commented doubtfully.

The Major staggered up, bowed under the weight of the proscenium arch, with Andy acting as a red flag at the other end.

Between them they stowed the equipment in *Pauline*'s large cabin.

Ross, at the tiller of *Sea Rider,* with the Major and Holly beside him, soon found the *Pauline* drawing away rapidly.

" She's a grayhound, all right," he remarked. " What a snorting job. Though I wouldn't change *Sea Rider* for any other craft under the sun. She got us out of Corrievreckan, and that takes a lot of forgetting."

" She wouldn't have done if Deathshead could have helped it," Holly remarked, waving to the now distant figures of Sergeant Dryden and Andy on the landing stage. " I wonder what he's doing."

Ross's smile faded.

" I'll bet he knows just what we're doing."

Holly shivered. " At least we know he's not in *Sea Rider.* And he can't be stowed away in the *Pauline.*"

It was nearly four o'clock when the panting *Sea Rider* came up with the *Pauline,* already bobbing at anchor, and grated on Fluran's sandy shore.

" Where've you been? " Charles Gordon cried, catching Holly in his arms. " We got a terrible shock when that spanking launch drew in first, and with a policeman on board too! "

" Daddy! " Holly said severely. " You're not to sneer at

Sea Rider. She's little but she's good."

Leonie had a handsome tea waiting.

"I'm glad we're giving the show in the open, not in a stuffy hall," Holly remarked.

"I'm looking forward to it," Ross said. "The Commander's going to do two shows, one for the leisured classes in the afternoon and the other in the evening for the workers."

"She's an optimist," Holly grinned. "The total population of Fluran's only about forty."

"And all forty mad with excitement," remarked Leonie. "There won't be much work done tomorrow. I don't think any of them have ever been to a cinema, let alone a stage show."

And the stage show really started after breakfast the next morning, when the Major and Mrs. Lumley, who had spent the night with an overawed Miss Ethnie turned out onto a flat piece of ground by the ferry to erect the proscenium arch. The mails came and went unnoticed. Iain, the postman, even had to pick up the newspapers himself for the first time. Miss Ethnie, greatly daring, wrote "Out of Order" on a post card and propped it up against the telephone, and then sank deeper into crime by lending the post office for a dressing room.

Holly, as a Highland princess, strove harder than she had ever done before to please her simple, eager audience. Before her on the grass sat all her Fluran friends — Iain, his post bag forgotten, Miss Ethnie wearing her best lace cap, Jamie, and old Niall the shepherd, grave and upright. Especially did she try for Niall, because she knew he expected much of her.

Their audience did not wait to clap at the end. They just ran through the arch and fell on the Globe Players.

" Och, 'twas braw," sighed Iain. " Nobody has ever troubled tae bring Fluran sich a treat."

The Commander, radiant with delight, yet with tears in her eyes, bowed graciously.

Charles Gordon smiled at Holly: " They're scared of her but they adore her. She's a great woman."

The Commander swept through her admirers and advanced on the dressing room.

" You're all free until this evening," she beamed. " I have consented by popular request to work through the whole of my repertoire for these most charming people. Do just as you like."

" Let's go for a run," Holly whispered to Hugh Tarbet. " We've got masses of time."

She glanced toward Ross, who was talking to Niall. Tarbet followed her look and nodded.

" He's a fine figure of a lad, especially in the Highland dress. Looks as if he's worn it all his life. Your producer's made a wonderful job of it. Absolutely correct in every detail. But the lad puts the finishing touch. I wouldn't mind having a son like that."

Holly bit her lip. " He's nobody's son now, Mr. Tarbet. He's all on his own. He was wishing only the other day someone would write to him."

" He's got you," Tarbet remarked.

" Yes. He's always got me."

She turned away. " Would you ask him to hurry up and get changed, please? "

Tarbet came back with Ross.

" We're going for a cruise, I hear," Ross grinned. " But I'm not going to get out of this costume and into it again. The Commander has to pour me in."

" Let him come as he is," suggested Tarbet.

" Don't encourage him," Pud grinned. " He's getting much too attached to those whiskers and soon won't take them off at all. I wonder what the Oceanic will say. Can't you see the headlines: ' First Cabin Boy to Wear a Beard '? "

" Well, I'm not going to change either," Holly declared. The Commander had to sew me into mine. You only got poured into yours. Come on, Pud," and she started down the stone slope to the landing stage.

" No, thanks," Pud said firmly. " The sea and I don't agree. I'm going to stay on dry land. I haven't got over that horrid trip from Fort William yet."

" Where to? " Tarbet said. " We've got plenty of fuel and a maximum speed of twenty knots."

Ross looked at Holly. " Shall we? " he murmured.

" Yes, I think we can trust him," Holly replied pretending to examine Tarbet closely.

" Hey, what's all this? " he exclaimed. " I'm the one who usually does the inspecting! "

Holly put on a solemn face. " Are you trustworthy, discreet, and able to keep a secret? If so, we are prepared to spill the beans."

" Hullo! What beans? What have you two been up to? Not robbery with violence, I hope. A full confession, please! But, first of all, where are we heading?"

" The Soise group," Ross said.

" H'm. Not a place I should choose for a pleasure trip myself."

" Wait until you've heard all," Holly said seriously. " Go on, Ross."

To the accompanying throb of *Pauline*'s engines, Ross related the whole story of the casebook, and all they had found out since Holly started it on the way to Inverkenneth.

Tarbet's pleasant rugged face was thoughtful when he had finished.

" It's all most interesting and most ingenious. I could do with you two in my department. And it explains several things too," he added. " I'd already heard some bits about Dundas. For a start, he's been trying to get his mother certified as insane and unable to control her affairs."

" So he could take over," put in Holly.

Tarbet nodded. " It looks like it now I've heard your story. Also Chandler, the personnel manager, says he's been shouting his mouth off at the works about how the French and Spanish bauxite markets had better watch out."

" Then it is bauxite he's after," Ross exclaimed.

" Looks like it," Tarbet nodded. " He'll be a rich man if he manages to win his mother over. And prove Trillsean belongs to his family."

" But of course it does. Doesn't it? " Holly said.

Tarbet glanced at the compass. " The estates were returned to their original owners in 1784," he remarked.

" The original owner had gone south to be hanged with Fireflaught! " Holly exclaimed.

" But you say they escaped to France where the original owner — your Ross E, as you call him — got married and had a son," Tarbet put in.

Holly paused. " Then Ross is — "

" Yes, if we can prove it somehow," Tarbet replied. " And you say Fireflaught was killed at Trafalgar."

" That's right. It was all in the letter from Samuel Kilbride. I think Fireflaught would have been pleased to die like that. Even his name sounds like the flash of a sword," Holly said thoughtfully.

Tarbet smiled. " It's strange you should say that. It does

mean a flash. Not of a sword though. It's old Scots for a flash of lightning."

"That's funny," Holly exclaimed. "Do you remember Mad Mollie said she'd be in the dark without the lightning's beams? And when I told you, you said how could there be lightning in an underground cave?"

Ross nodded thoughtfully, his eyes on the rippling water.

Tarbet reduced speed. "Here we are. The Soise group right ahead."

Holly's eyes went straight to Trillsean, green and empty in the afternoon sunlight, crowned with seabirds and the scent of the white rose.

"Hurdie's boat's off Soise," Ross said, shading his eyes. "I thought he said he was going trouting in Loch Kenneth and wouldn't be back."

Hugh Tarbet cruised along the outer ring of the Clach Mallach and glanced at them. "I suppose you two want to have another look at your cave," he said. "The tide's out. You'll be able to walk in this time."

"Aren't you coming too?" Holly asked.

He grinned. "Policemen on holiday don't go poking their noses in where they aren't wanted. No, it's your own private job. I'll stick around just outside this arch and see if I can catch something worth having for supper. And don't forget to wedge your stone open this time."

"We'll be all right," Ross nodded. "We've got our escape hatch through the roof."

Tarbet held *Pauline* off the rocks while they jumped down.

"You can use this hurricane lamp. It'll just about give you enough light to see where you're going. Don't catch that beard on fire. And don't be long."

Hand in hand Ross and Holly entered the cave.

"There's the bit of mooring rope," Ross said. "Still hanging on the bit of rock."

They had entered the passage. Ross lighted the lamp. It threw a small circle of light around their feet as they climbed the rock-strewn slope.

Ross put his hand on the swinging stone. It turned as smoothly as it had done before. The blackness of the cave yawned in front.

"Let's walk straight ahead this time." Holly said in a low voice. She laughed nervously. "I can't seem to talk loud in here."

"I know," Ross said. "It seems wrong to come and disturb it somehow. I felt the same when we came in the first time. As if there's some sort of presence in the air."

The circle of light showed them a rocky floor.

"I don't think there's anything here after all," Holly whispered.

"Yes, there is. Look at this."

The lamplight had fallen on a heavy wooden stool and beyond the stool a roughly hewn table.

"Then he really did live here once," Holly breathed. "Ross! There's something on the table. At the far end. A piece of paper fixed to the wood with a dirk."

Ross stood the lamp on the table. "I hardly like to touch it." He hesitated. "There's something written in Gaelic."

"Take the knife out," begged Holly. "See if you can read it."

Ross laid his hand on the shaft and pulled. "That was driven home by someone either in a rage or a hurry," he muttered. "The blade was in nearly to the hilt."

"Try to read it," Holly whispered urgently. She stared at his face lighted by the circle of light and saw its muscles tighten. "Do you think you can?"

"Yes, I think so." His voice sounded strangled. "'My beloved Trillsean, I go out to die. I — bequeath you to the winds and waves. My — spirit shall return to — accuse my betrayers. Go prick them, little white rose.'"

They stared at each other across the table.

"Poor, poor Old Villain," Holly faltered.

Ross laid the paper down gently. "He did go out to die but it was in a strange place far from home. And the white rose has been pricking his betrayers ever since."

"You mean — the people on Soise?" Holly stammered.

"I reckon that's why they've got the blight, as Hurdie put it. Witch doctors in Africa can put that kind of curse on people and it really works. Or appears to work. Fear is usually at the bottom of it. The people of Soise have inherited the curse from their ancestors. They must have had a hand in the Old Villain's capture."

"There's something else on the ground," Holly said. "Under the table. Something that shines."

Ross bent down. "It's a stone like the ones in that shop in Inverness."

"A plaid brooch," Holly whispered. "A silver rose with a cairngorm in the middle. Perhaps he dropped it when — Let's see if there's any more of him here. I think we're near the other side."

They moved from the table into the shadows.

"Yes, you're right," Ross murmured. "Here's the opposite end of the cave."

He raised the lamp.

They both stared at the wall, transfixed.

The light had fallen on the portrait of a Highlander, in the full dress of a clan chieftain, his bonneted auburn head with its eagle's feathers tossed back, his amber eyes staring down at them with a proud and careless glance.

" Fireflaught," Holly breathed, her blood cold. " What is Fireflaught doing in the Old Villain's cave? "

Ross had taken one look and involuntarily hung his head as if in homage. He nodded dumbly to the base of the picture.

Holly dropped her eyes to the titles of Sir Henry Raeburn's friend.

ROSS FIREFLAUGHT
MACAUDREY OF MACAUDREY
LANTERN OF THE NORTH
LAIRD OF SOISE AND TRILLSEAN

She stared stupidly up again at the auburn hair and amber eyes.

" There weren't two. Only one. Fireflaught is the Old Villain. He belongs to you. He is you. And it wasn't an E on the snuffbox. It was an F. For Fireflaught."

Ross lips were trembling as he nodded.

" And now I know how Dundas recognized you," Holly whispered. " By your eyes. And by your likeness to that picture. You were wearing a beard when he first saw you. Like Fireflaught up there."

" Do you remember Mad Mollie talked about the Lantern as if the Lantern was a person? " Ross said softly.

" Yes. And she said she'd be in the dark without the lightning's beams. Fireflaught means flash of lightning," Holly breathed. " Poor Mad Mollie's been staring into those eyes too. I believe he got called Fireflaught because they shine so."

The rustle of a falling stone made them both turn sharply. Ross raised the lamp. A harshly drawn breath cut through the darkness.

" Ah, MacAudrey, we meet again! But this time it shall be the last."

The light illumined the face of Murdo Dundas, convulsed with hate. He advanced with deadly purpose toward Ross, who laid the lamp on the table and turned to face him.

Dundas sprang forward. Ross took the full weight of the savage body on his shoulder. The force of the impact threw them both to the ground.

Holly gave a wild scream. Frozen with terror, she watched Ross's silent struggle to stop his head from being beaten to pulp against the heavy legs of the table.

Dundas clawed and writhed and tore in his frantic effort to get at Ross's throat. At last youth and hard sea training began to tell, in spite of the hampering costume. With a supreme effort Ross threw Dundas clear and sprang up. Dundas twisted to his feet, blood dripping from his forehead. Again he advanced upon Ross, who stood watching and waiting. Holly tried to scream a warning. Only a strangled murmur escaped her lips. Dundas flicked his head around for a fraction of a second and in that second Ross had dived.

Dundas swung through the shadows in a wide arc, hit the rocky floor, and lay still. And then once more he had dragged to his feet, swaying and bleeding. Once more he staggered forward.

And then a terrible scream tore across the darkness from the direction of the shaft.

" Th' Lantern! " shrieked the voice of Mad Mollie. " He's come doon frae th' wall. Dinna y touch him, ye divil."

She threw herself on Dundas. He thrust her away savagely and she fell in a shuddering heap. He whirled around, seized the stool, and swung it. Holly recoiled. Ross tried to shield his head with his arms.

But before Dundas could strike, Mad Mollie was up. She caught up the dirk from the table and with the towering force of a maniac buried it to the hilt in her son's back.

" A Dundas betrayed a MacAudrey! Now let a Dundas die for it! " she screamed.

The swaying body swung around on its heel. The stool crashed down onto Mad Mollie's head. Mother and son sank to the floor together.

A moment of frozen silence. Then Ross and Holly crept toward the two bodies.

" What shall we do? " she whispered, her face half buried against her arm. " Are they —? "

" Having any trouble? " Hugh Tarbet's voice echoed through the darkness. " Are you all right, you two? "

" C-come here quick," Ross faltered.

They heard Tarbet's feet crunching rapidly across the floor.

" B-be careful," Ross said. " Don't come any farther. Dundas and his mother are lying by the table."

Tarbet shone his torch down, uttered a sharp sound, and gently turned the bodies over.

" He's gone. But the old woman's still alive. Raise her up. I'll get some water."

Ross bent down and put his arm tenderly under Mad Mollie's shoulders.

" She saved me," he whispered to Holly, who had taken hold of the poor creature's hand.

Mad Mollie's sunken eyes opened. She looked up into Ross's face with an expression of fear and adoration.

" I'm offered up, MacAudrey," she muttered. " All sins be washed away. I've paid ma debt, ma dear acquaintance."

Ross bent down and laid a tender kiss on the forehead. The twisted face relaxed into smiling peace.

"Don't look any more, old girl," he whispered to Holly. "She's gone to where Fireflaught is waiting."

Holly turned away in silent tears.

Tarbet came swiftly toward them with the water.

"It's no good, sir," Ross said. "She's —"

Tarbet touched the body gently and nodded.

"Yes, I'm afraid so. There's nothing more we can do for either of them. I'll have to contact the station. But I'll drop you two on Fluran first."

Holly turned and raised her eyes to Fireflaught. He seemed to be looking straight down at poor Mad Mollie with the warm glance she had loved and fought so hard to save.

17

CALM SEA AND A PLEASANT VOYAGE

PAULINE's engines vibrated with a thunderous growl as Tarbet put her full-out back toward the mainland.

They were silent for a long time, overcome by the gathering storm of climax that had at last crashed so violently over their heads. Holly watched Trillsean fading to a square smudge on the horizon.

" Less than an hour ago we were on our way. They were — both alive then."

Ross pressed her hand and stared at the wide wall of water piling past the prow. " At least they're not frightened of anything any more. Perhaps the curse of that old betrayal has died with Dundas. Maybe it'll pick up a bit now on Soise."

" It'll be up to you, MacAudrey," remarked Tarbet. " You are about to come into a rather solid inheritance."

Ross flushed at the title.

" He doesn't care about the bauxite. He's got the Merchant Navy," Holly replied.

" I care for it enough to hope it will help me to wipe that pinched look off their faces," Ross replied grimly.

Tarbet nodded. " I don't think the real ownership of the group will take much proving with that portrait and the rest of the evidence you've found. I've never in my life seen such a likeness. What a blessing conditions were right in that cave! If it had been damp, I doubt if the portrait would have been in good enough condition to be used as evidence. No wonder Dundas was so anxious to know if his mother had seen you. She would have recognized you at once for who you were."

" But he did too, didn't he? " Holly put in.

" I know that. But he realized that all hope of winning her over to the idea of mining Trillsean would have gone if she had seen him. She would have sworn Fireflaught had returned to claim his birthright."

" I reckon it was she who was the MacAudreys' guardian angel. She did what she could for them, weak as she was against that ambitious devil." Ross's voice shook at the remembrance of poor Mad Mollie.

" I don't know that she was so weak," Tarbet responded. " She fought him and headed him off just long enough. When I saw him on the top of Trillsean having a quick look around before he disappeared down the shaft and then the old woman come tearing after him and disappearing too, I guessed some dirty business was afoot."

" I'm surprised he risked it with you watching him," Ross said.

" He didn't know I was watching. I had my back turned and was busy pulling in a nice fat bass."

" But you said you saw him go down the shaft," Holly exclaimed.

" Correct. I have the *Pauline*'s previous owners and their love of nice bright chromium to thank for that little trick. I propped this ghastly thing up on the bench."

He pointed to a large chromium-plated mirror.

" And got a very adequate and authentic view of all that

was going on behind me. I reckon he pinched Hurdie's boat and came over in that."

He stood up and reduced speed.

" Here's Fluran coming up ahead. I can see my little mascot waiting for us."

The Commander still wore her glow of triumph when Holly stepped onto the causeway. Miss Ethnie had a handsome high tea laid out in front of the post office. Iain still sat with his eyes glued to the back cloth of sea and cloud through the prosenium arch.

Holly sighed. " It all looks so beautifully normal. And I do feel so shaky."

Pud grinned. " And you look awfully pale. What ever's the matter? You should have stayed on dry land like me. Come and have some tea supper. And try Miss Ethnie's bannocks. They may be better even than your Mr. Bunker's."

Holly followed her up the causeway. At the top Pud turned and stared. " Hullo! Isn't Hugh coming as well? No, he isn't. Well, of all the — He's backing and turning for the mainland. We'll have to do the evening show without our one-man crowd of villagers. And what's wrong with our fake chieftain? He looks as if he's been fighting an army singlehanded! "

Holly smiled wanly. " Pud, he's not a fake. We've just found out he really is a chieftain. He's the Chief of the MacAudrey clan."

" W-what? " Pud stammered. " You're kidding! "

This time Holly really managed a laugh. " Honest. Let's find a quiet corner and I'll tell you."

Pud's freckled face was rounder than ever when Holly had finished.

" D-do you mean to say all that has happened since you left here after the first show? On just a sea trip? "

Holly nodded. " And, Pud, just think of the awful long, dull hours we shall soon be enduring back at school. Math and civics and all that stuff."

" And we've got a new chemistry mistress who absolutely loaths me," Pud added gloomily.

" Our math mistress feels worse than that about me," Holly sighed. " Well, at least we can say our holiday's been worth the fare. I shall tell Daddy so. He always grumbles terribly about the fare."

A further sensation greeted the audience at the evening program when the leading man appeared, bruised and bandaged and with a torn costume but with his usual resolute smile.

" I can't help it, Ross," Holly confessed solemnly afterward, when they were taking off their make-up. "I feel a new kind of respect for you now you're a clan chief. Same as I feel for the Cock o' the North, the chief of the Gordons. I hope it's not going to make any difference to us."

Ross shouted with laughter. " I'll show you if it'll make any difference! " and seizing the " wet white " from the make-up box, he held it threateningly over her head.

" No, Ross, no! " she shrieked, trying to grab his arm.

Ross smiled grimly and held on. Holly tried to kick him. He swung around and the bottle of wet white emptied itself over the floor of the post office.

" What exactly is going on? " inquired the Commander, sailing majestically in. " Wet white is not a shampoo, dear children. Ross, let go of Holly's hair. And get down and mop the floor."

Holly gasped. " Let me do it, Mrs. Lumley. You can't ask him! He's the MacAudrey of MacAudrey! "

" I'm not asking him, I'm telling him," replied the Commander. " And I don't care if he's an archbishop. Those who spill have to mop up."

The story of Trillsean was the sole topic of conversation at the fish supper provided by Hugh Tarbet and again at breakfast the next morning. Holly was sitting on the grass outside the house sucking a piece of grass and staring sadly at her casebook when Iain came striding down Cairnmor waving his stick and two letters. " Thon's for th' guidman," he said, " and thon's for th' wee lad."

" Daddy! " Holly shouted. " A letter from Aunt Lottie. But who on earth's writing to Robert? "

" 'Tis not for th' weest lad, 'tis for th' wee lad," Iaîn replied patiently.

" Oh, I see," Holly said. " For Ross. I'll give it to him."

Iain looked doubtful. " 'Tis agin th' regulations. Aye, but I'll let th' regulations go hang th' day. I canna bide. I'm helpin' th' Prince o' Women wi' her packin'."

He stumped off. Charles Gordon grinned. " The Major's got a rival. He'll have to look out. This isn't from Charlotte. It's from a Mrs. Warburton."

" It must be. It's Aunt Lottie's writing."

" Maybe. But Aunt Lottie is now Mrs. Frederick Warburton. She says it's all your fault, Holly."

" A-Aunt Lottie — m-married? " Holly stammered.

" To a man connected with some church at Deal. I'm surprised at Charlotte. Practically an elopement."

" Daddy, I'm not surprised," she replied, shaking her head. " Aunt Lottie is a gay dog in some ways."

Her father opened his mouth but she hastened on. " She won't be able to send me my ten shillings back if I buy her a wedding present, will she, Ross? Why, what's the matter? "

Ross was staring at his letter with a flushed face.

"From the Oceanic," he said quietly. "'Please join *Portland Bay,* Tilbury, August 31, 6 P.M.'"

"*P-Portland Bay?*" faltered Holly. "Has it come at last? Wasn't that — ?"

"Yes, Dad's ship," Ross said with bewildered pride. "This letter's been following me around for about three weeks. Look at the envelope. I'll have to go at once."

"B-but your — estates?" stammered Holly.

Everyone laughed. "When it's all gone through the official channels, as they say in my department," Hugh Tarbet smiled, "you can safely leave it to me. I'm on the spot. That is, if you care to, Son."

Tarbet looked down at Ross's flushed face.

"I shall be happy to oblige in the capacity of a parent if you should ever feel the need of one," he said gently.

"But Fireflaught! You can't leave Fireflaught there!" pursued Holly.

"I want your mother to have him, if he's mine to give," Ross said.

Leonie threw up her hands. "No, Ross! I couldn't bear to live with a Raeburn. I'd get an inferiority complex. He must go where he belongs. To Edinburgh."

"And talking of going," put in Charles Gordon, "where's the timetable? He'll have to step on it. Tilbury in two days, remember."

"All my kit's in the Globe," Ross exclaimed.

"This is where the *Pauline*'s speed comes in useful," Hugh Tarbet smiled. "I'll take him on first and you can follow in *Sea Rider*. We'll all give him a grand send-off. This is somewhat of an occasion."

Holly watched *Pauline* heading away for the mainland and flew up to say good-by to Niall.

"I've got to go, Niall. I'm bad at saying farewells," she faltered.

Niall pressed her hand. "Ye'll be back. Ye hae mony lang and bonny years before ye."

He felt in the pocket of his old leather waistcoat. "D'ye ken whit a bawbee is? In th' auld times a mon and a woman would gie each other a bawbee as a bond and pledge o' undyin' affection. 'Tis for ye. Tae dae whit ye like wi'."

Holly took the little twisted sixpence. "Thank you, Niall. He — had to go quickly. He was sorry, because he liked you."

"Aye," Niall said. "He'll make a rare mon. Th' Gaelic's in thon laddie's blood. I didna hae tae learn him. He juist kenned it. He's nae Englishmon, that laddie."

"No," Holly said. "He's a Highlander, the truest of the true."

And never was a Highlander speeded on his outward way by a more devoted band of followers.

The Commander, in her black hat and cloak, caused a sensation among the porters as she headed the procession along the platform.

"Au revoir, not good-by, my dearest boy," she said, wiping her eyes under cover of the hat. "Don't eat too much rice in the Far East. It's bad for the figure. Bumble, cheer yourself up. You look like an undertaker."

She stepped aside as the porters began banging the doors. Ross, back in his uniform, leaned out of the carriage window, gazing down at Holly.

"You — look terribly clean," she said tremulously. "Let's hope they don't give you the coal bunkers to clean out for your first job."

Ross smiled. "The *Portland Bay* burns oil. By the way,

we owe the Northern Lighthouse Board a canful."

Holly tried to laugh. The porters were coming nearer.

Ross held out his hand. " Good-by, my very best friend," he said softly.

Without letting go of his hand, Holly felt in her pocket for the twisted sixpence.

" What is it, dear? " Ross said.

" Just an old Scottish custom," Holly whispered.

The train began to move. She stepped back, tears in her eyes and a smile on her lips, and saluted smartly.

" A calm sea and a pleasant voyage, MacAudrey. And may the Admiral of All Fleets go with you."